ANA

Gary Hope

"Ana," by Gary Hope. ISBN 978-1-949756-64-7 (softcover); 978-1-949756-65-4 (eBook).

Published 2019 by Virtualbookworm.com Publishing Inc., P.O. Box 9949, College Station, TX , 77842, US.

For my beautiful wife

And

All those people who believe in magic

‖‖‖

PREVIOUS BOOKS BY GARY HOPE

It's Too Late to Die Young Now

Abbey

The Girl From Tir-na-nOg

The Confluence

Niamh

Friends

Left of the Middle

I wish you peace when the cold winds blow
 Warmed by the fire's glow
I wish you comfort in the lonely time
And arms to hold you when you ache inside

I wish you hope when things are going bad
Kind words when times are sad
I wish you shelter from the raging wind
Cooling waters at the fever's end

 I wish you peace when times are hard
The light to guide you through the dark
And when storms are high and your dreams are low

I wish you the strength to let love grow,
I wish you the strength to let love flow

Leadon & Davis

ONE

I'm a newspaper columnist for the *Salt Lake City Tribune*. I don't live in Salt Lake City, however. Too many fake Mormons up there for me. I live down here in the desert in a little place called Moab, Utah, where all the citizens are good and righteous jack-Mormons. They don't pretend to be anything but themselves . . . heck, some of them are even Baptists. When I started working for the paper I lived in SLC, but quickly got out of that quagmire of big city life, high rent, and low morals.

Whereas Utah has the highest literacy rate in the country, it also has the highest rate of online porn subscriptions in the United States. Plus, I couldn't breathe up there—too much industrial pollution, people pollution, and intellectual snobbery. So, after a few years of building my newspaper column's popularity, the editors allowed me to move to my present home out here in the middle of nowhere—Moab. I send in my column by email and enjoy my life out here in the remote wilderness . . . in a two-bedroom condo about a half-mile from the Moab brewery. I like the wilderness for sure, but I also like the conveniences of civilization.

My newspaper column started as an information outlet for people asking all sorts of questions: about living in Utah, cooking (of which I knew nothing), camping, traveling, Mormonism (of which I know next-to-nothing), sports, recreation, books, or anything else. I was a sports guy originally. I wrote about the professional and college teams here in the Beehive State. But my columns started becoming more popular than the sports scores and started taking a life of their own. Soon I was promoted (or demoted, as the case may be) to columnist and one of the new guys took over my sports duties. Actually, a lady took them over and her picture in the sports pages made the scores look a whole lot better to look at than mine ever did.

Generally, I'll answer the questions from people who write or email in, or I'll just extrapolate on any subject that gets me thinking that particular day. I try not to be mean or cruel, but often, I can't help myself. As with this letter which came from a lady living in the suburbs of SLC: "Noah, what can I do to keep the javelinas from eating my petunias each night? Signed, Margaret."

My answer: "Dear Margaret, first you'll have to move to Arizona where javelinas actually live (There are none in Utah.) Then plant a field full of prickly pear cactus, since that's their favorite food, and then they'll probably ignore your petunias. If this doesn't work, please let me know."

I'm single, never been married, never even been engaged. Why? That's a good question. One I don't have an adequate answer for. I love women, sometimes too much, sometimes probably not enough. At any rate, it's just never worked out for me. Now, I'm out here in the middle of nowhere, my chances of matrimonial bliss seem pretty darned slim. But, that's okay-- I've got the desert, the mountains, the canyons, the buttes and mesas, the rivers and streams, the monoclines and inclines, the washes and . . . who am I kidding? I'm lonely—but happy. There are women out here in the desert. Good, stout, hard-working, hard-drinking, river guides, hikers, bikers, bakers, and candlestick makers. Some are even attractive in their own unique ways. Most are married, or don't want to be married, or you wouldn't want to marry them . . . if you know what I mean.

Now, finally, I'll come to the point of my little story here: I've fallen in love. Yes, me. Curmudgeon extraordinaire. Someone who's never satisfied, never contented, unsatiated and insatiable at the same time. I have found someone! Of course, I've never actually met this woman. Don't even know what she looks like, or how old she is, or anything else about her—except her brain, which I love. I don't even know her name: She always uses "Ana" when she signs off her emails, which I'm pretty sure is not her real name. Why do I think that? Because when I asked her to tell me her last name, she said it was Lytic. An odd last name I thought until I said her first and last names out loud: Ana Lytic.

But that's her story and she's sticking to it. This is what I do know about Ana: She's definitely a woman; she lives in North Carolina; she's smart; she has a good sense of humor; and she's very, very vague. She visited Salt Lake City once and read my column one day when I answered this question: "Noah, I have a friend who sometimes doesn't act like a friend. How can I be sure she's a true friend? Signed, Ava."

I use the pen name Noah for my column because Noah had a lot of patience—it took him 120 years to build an ark for apparently no reason—except that God told him to. I also have to have a lot of patience with my readers—plus, I like the name, Noah. My answer: "Dear Ava, friendship is like peeing on yourself. Everyone can see that you've peed on yourself, but only you get the warm feeling from it. If you don't get that warm feeling, she's not your friend."

Ana liked that answer. She emailed me and told me so, and that started our relationship. She soon went back to her home in North Carolina, though she won't tell me where, and continues to read my columns online. She writes to tell me how smart I am, or how crazy I am, or how wrong I am. And I write back—and dream of Ana . . . oh, sweet Ana.

ᎶᎶᎶ

"Noah: My neighbor is suing me over some trivial matter regarding our boundary line. He would like me just to settle with him out of court, but I want a jury to hear my story and let them decide. Who do you think is right? Signed, Wade."

"Dear Wade: Here's what I think: If you go to court, you are putting yourself into the hands of twelve people who weren't smart enough to get out of jury duty. Is that what you want?"

"Noah: Who are you voting for in the next election? Signed, Earl."

"Dear Earl: I'm not voting and here's why: if voting made any difference, they wouldn't let us vote, now would they?"

"Noah: Sometimes you're just hard-headed and stubborn! Why can't you be more open-minded about things? Signed, Pam."

3

"Dearest, sweet, innocent Pam: Here's why: There is a distinct difference between having an open mind and having a hole in your head from which your brain leaks out! I hope that answers your question."

⌒‿⌒‿⌒

"Noah: I'm writing to tell you that I'm sick and tired of your blustering and pontificating about everything and always thinking your right. You're not always right, in fact, your seldom right. I wish I had the right to be heard by all these readers so they could hear the truth once in a while, and not you're version of it. Signed, Olin T. Seymore."

"Dear: Mr. Olin T. Seymore, First of all, congratulations on your creative uses of the words 'your' and 'you're.' Second, the right to be heard, such as you desire, does not automatically include the right to be taken seriously. So be glad you're you—and not me."

⌒‿⌒‿⌒

"Dear, Noah: I was wondering if a person had their brain removed by aliens, yet their heart continued to beat, would they technically be considered alive or dead? Just curious . . . what do you think? Signed, D. Lusk."

"Dear D: I've thought long and hard about your dilemma, and here's my conclusion: When you are dead, you don't actually know that you are dead. It is only apparent to the others around you. It's the same when you're stupid. Hope this clears things up for you."

⌒‿⌒‿⌒

I get to answer all these questions, live in the desert, and walk around my condo all day in my underwear. Who's got it made? Me!

I usually get an email from Ana each evening. Sometimes she responds to something I've said in the column or corrects some injustice she thinks I've communicated. Mostly, though, she just writes to me, tells about her anonymous life—anonymous to me, that is. She never discusses anything too personal because she doesn't want to take the chance that I could trace her down. I've tried, though not too hard. I suppose I could hire some computer nerds to back trace her email account and somehow figure out who she is and where she lives. But why? If she wanted me to know, she'd tell me.

There are some days I think I don't want to know. I just want to keep the dream alive. I'm afraid I might find out Ana's married, or eleven years old, or ninety-eight years old, and have my dreams ruined! I couldn't handle that. You see, I think I'm addicted to Ana. I sit in front of the computer each night waiting for her email, staring blindly at the screen—cursing it, spitting at it, kicking it, berating it, but none of it does any good. Finally, her message comes and I read it five times, six times, seven times until I have memorized every word of it.

I quickly type her back a response, usually long and full of amorous aphorisms. She never replies. She only writes the one time each evening—never twice. Never answers my replies no matter how languid and longing they may be. This only makes me want her more. Or, want the idea of her more. Maybe Ana is an ugly witch of a woman with warts on her nose and black fingernails. Heck, at this point, I don't think I'd care. For now, I'll play along and be and do, whatever Ana wants me to.

TWO

I think my columns have been successful and kept me employed because I'm basically honest and a little humorous with people. The paper is so full of serious, dreadful news and events that, I think, most people enjoy a break in the drudgery of daily news. My goal is to always be sincere, even if I don't always mean it.

"Noah: I enjoy reading your columns each morning with my coffee. I was wondering, are you a morning person like me? Signed, Hazel."

"Dear Hazel: There are two kinds of people in the world. Those who wake up in the morning and say, 'Good morning, Lord.' And there are those who wake up in the morning and say, 'Good Lord, it's morning.' And that's my answer."

"Noah: I consider myself an average person, certainly not smarter than everyone else, like you sometimes think you are. And all my friends are average as well—no snobbery in my group of friends. I was wondering if you try to hang around with snobs like yourself, or normal average people like us? Signed, Ellen."

"Ellen, dear sweet, Ellen: Thank you for the kind note. In answer to your question, I don't really hang around with anyone—I'm mostly a loner. I was very glad to read that you, however, do have a group of average friends to spend your time with. But, Ellen, you do understand this, don't you: Half the people you know in your average group of friends are BELOW average—right?"

"Noah: I just got laid off from my job. I'm feeling pretty bummed about it. I know I'll find something else, but I can't help but feel a little depressed and sad. Any words of wisdom to brighten my day? Signed, Bud."

"Dear Bud: Sorry to hear of your job loss; that's never an easy thing to cope with. I wish I had some magic words to make everything better, but I don't. Time seems to be the best and only solution—that and finding another job, obviously. However, I will offer this . . . what we see usually depends on what we're looking for. If your ship doesn't come in soon—swim out to it! And good luck, Bud."

"Noah: I'm ninety-six years old and still in good enough health to type this message. I know I don't have much longer on this earth, but I still dream of things—all sorts of things. My children tell me I should live in the present and stop my foolish dreams of traveling and adventure. What do you say? Signed, Conrad."

"Conrad, my friend: Excuse my language, but your children sound like butt-holes. In my opinion, people who don't have dreams don't have much! Keep on dreaming, my friend, and don't worry about old age-- it doesn't last that long anyway."

"Noah: I cannot believe the majority of people in our state voted for this idiot we have as a governor. He's crazy! Certainly, the good people of Utah cannot be this blind to elect such an incompetent fool as this. What do you think? Signed, Allen."

"Allen: What you seem to misunderstand about our entire electoral process is that we, here in America, DO NOT have government by the majority. As Thomas Jefferson so eloquently described it, we have government by the majority of those who PARTICIPATE! Those who actually vote. So, until the masses rise up and get out of their lazy boy chairs and leave their Starbucks coffee shop and actually vote in an election, we will continue to be ruled only by those who do vote, not by the majority."

⌣⌣⌣

This last response of mine about voting brought about a three-page response from Ana. Unfortunately for me, she only discussed the electoral process, democracy, and the apparent numbness of the masses toward their own destiny. Not a word about how much she misses me, nor how she treasures my comments and friendship, nor how she is so looking forward to the day we get together—nothing! Can you believe it?

⌣⌣⌣

"Noah: I just read that the life expectancy here in Utah is the highest in the country. I don't think we should be publicizing that! I mean, we don't want all these foreigners moving here just because they think they might live longer, do we? It's not our fault that the rest of the country isn't as good as we are. Our life is special here and we shouldn't be jeopardizing it by inviting everyone in the world to move here. Can't they fix their own problems? What is the main cause of death in the world, Noah? Whatever it is, that's what they need to work on, not moving here to Utah. Am I right? Signed, a concerned citizen."

"Dear concerned citizen: You make a good point about the rest of the world. I did a lot of research about this issue and found that Death is the Number 1 killer in the entire world—including Utah. And, alarmingly for those of us in Utah, I found that Life is sexually transmitted. So be careful out there, and I hope that clears things up for you."

⌣⌣⌣

"Noah: I read in your paper that unemployment has risen again in our state. That's very distressing. I'm sick of seeing all the hobos and drifters standing on the corners begging for money. Can't something be done about that? Isn't there some sort of program that can teach these worthless people a skill and make them useful so they'll quit bothering us? After all, remember the old saying, 'Give a man a fish and he'll be happy for one day, but teach him to fish and he'll be productive forever.' Right? Signed, Jimmy."

"Jimmy, Jimmy, Jimmy: I appreciate your concern for our homeless and unemployed population. I remember that old saying that you quoted about fishing, however, I found a more recent quote that fits today's landscape a lot better: 'Give a person a fish and you feed them for a day. Teach a person to use the internet and they won't bother you for weeks, months, maybe even years.' What do you think, Jimmy?"

ⓒⓒⓒ

The work week is now over and I'm off on my weekend hike here in the desert. I usually take a different trail each week and test the limits of my endurance (as long as I'm back before the Moab Brewery closes). This week I'm driving down to Canyonlands National Park to a trail I've seen before but never hiked. It's dangerous, treacherous, and full of thousand-foot drop-offs and quicksand entrapments that can snare even the most experienced hikers . . . on second thought, I'll think I'll just hike to Grandview Point and back. Easier and less dangerous maybe, but no less spectacular. That is why I moved here, to see things like this.

From the Grandview Point overlook, one can see where the canyons of the Colorado River and the Green River each snake through the canyon country towards their ultimate meeting point out in the middle of nowhere, in the back of beyond. I've been to the back of beyond before, several times, in fact. Each separate hike was like a fantasy trip most people never even dream of. Most of the time, I never meet other hikers—it's very remote and extremely gorgeous.

Before I ever moved down here, years and years ago, I hiked this trail down to the confluence of the two great rivers. At one point on the trail, you have to climb over some large boulders to get to the next part of the journey. It's mostly slickrock, with a few scattered pinyon pines and junipers spread throughout. I'm assuming someone, probably the National Park management, has piled up little stone cairns to help mark the way, so the casual (and experienced) hiker doesn't lose his way. At one point, just before the climb up the boulders, off to the side, almost out of sight, I made my own cairn of boulders about two feet high, on my first trip out here years ago.

In the middle of that little pile of rocks, I placed a Kennedy half dollar coin. Why? Because I wanted to. I wanted to come back years later and find that coin and remember the day I put it there. The only problem I had was that I could never find that cairn I had made. Each of my eight or nine trips out there, I searched and searched where I thought it was, but never found it. The hike to the confluence was about three to four hours long and it's hard to remember all parts of it. But still, I thought I'd find my little cairn. It couldn't have been washed away. The cairn I built was sturdy and out of the main wash area—plus, this region only gets about four inches of rain a year.

It couldn't have been knocked over because it was well off the trail and almost hidden behind one of the large boulders. But still, I couldn't find it—and I looked. And then today! I was hiking the trail and thinking about Ana. Those high, puffy clouds remind me of Ana lying on the beach (I've never seen Ana lying on the beach, mind you). Those high pinnacles over there remind me of Ana in high heels and a short dress, just as those red rock formations across the way remind me of Ana watching television. Then, I saw the cairn—my cairn! It shocked me back to reality. I went from thoughts and dreams of the illusory Ana to the immediate reality of JFK under those rocks.

As soon as I saw it, I knew it was mine. I had been looking in the wrong places before. My memory had failed me; this was indeed the right place. I remembered the cairn, the boulder, and the proximity to a lone juniper that I had been forgetting. Stupid me! I clambered over to the pile of rocks and waited for my hands to stop trembling. Then I slowly removed each stone, careful not to disturb the half dollar coin from its sixteen-year resting place. Halfway down, where the coin should be, it wasn't there. It must have slipped down through the rocks. After removing all the rocks—still no coin. The cairn was built on slickrock—no dirt whatsoever. I was heartbroken. I was almost sick. I picked up each rock and turned them over in my hand, thinking maybe my coin has somehow adhered to the bottom of one of the rocks. Nope. Nothing. I piled up the rocks as I'd found them and sadly continued my journey. No more thoughts of Ana, no thoughts of anything, except what in the world happened to my Kennedy half dollar.

THREE

I made it back to the Moab Brewery, but I couldn't find a seat because there were so many tourists there. What a bad day. So, I went home and the heavens opened, sunshine burst forth, and my gloomy thoughts of cairns and coins disappeared. I had two emails from Ana waiting for me. Two!

"Noah: I hope you're well. I wanted to tell you about a book I just finished reading; I think you might like it. Anyway, I'd like to hear how you feel about it. It's called Revenant. It's about a woman who dies and her spirit comes back to fall in love with a man she met years ago. Do you even think that's possible? To fall in love with someone like that? I'm interested to hear what you think.

"Also, I'm thinking of taking a vacation soon and wondered if you had any suggestions for me. Places I might be interested in or enjoy seeing. Let me know.

Thanks,

Ana"

And the second email,

"Noah: is that your real name?"

I read these two emails a thousand times. Maybe two thousand. And asked myself at least two thousand questions. Then I wrote Ana back—of course, she didn't answer. I told her my name, Noah, was as real as her name, Ana. Then I went online and ordered the book Revenant. Next, I emailed Ana again, even though I knew she wouldn't answer me:

"Ana: Did you know that the Noah in the Bible lived to be over 950 years old and that God only spoke to him five times during that entire span? That's how I feel with you sometimes.

Your friend,

Noah"

Of course, no answer that evening, but early the next morning I had an email when I turned on the computer.

"Noah: It's the possibility of having a dream come true that makes life interesting."

Sunday was a long, thought-provoking day. I didn't go to church (yes, I go to church), I didn't go out to eat, (yes, I can cook . . . a little), and I didn't watch television. I thought. It wore me out. I checked the computer about four thousand times, but no more messages from Ana. I'd have to wait until Monday.

Back at work: "Noah, I just found out that my husband has been having an affair for the last six months. I'm broken and don't know what to do. Why would he do that to me? Signed, Brokenhearted."

"My dearest, Brokenhearted: I am so very sorry. I wish I could do something to help or say something to help. But I can't. All I know is that humans aren't perfect. We hurt each other. We all need to find the ones worth suffering over. Only you will know that."

"Noah: Are you a Mormon? Signed, Joseph Smith."

"Dear Mr. Smith: Do men really live on the moon?"

"Noah: My husband has recently retired and all he seems to talk about now is dying. It's very depressing. Any ideas? Signed, Sara."

"Dear Sara: I'm sorry to hear about your husband's mindset. I've often seen in retired people the fear of death followed by the fear of living. Life isn't fair, Sara, but it's still good. Just keep reminding him that it's never too late to be happy. But it's all up to him and no one else. Good luck, Sara."

"Noah: I recently graduated from college and have some student debts that are building up. I can't seem to get them paid down very quickly. Will this debt hurt me? How much debt is okay and how much will the bank allow me to have? Signed, Seth."

"Dear Seth: You didn't tell me how much debt you have, but my answer is to pay it off as quickly as you can. Secondly, addressing your concerns with the bank—if you owe the bank $100, then you've got a problem. However, if you owe the bank $100 million, then the bank has a problem. It's all a matter of perception."

"Noah: My boyfriend broke up with me and started dating a floozy. It still hurts and I'm wondering how long it will continue to hurt. Since you're older than me, maybe you have some experience with this. I've always heard that time heals all wounds . . . I hope that's true. Signed, Amanda."

"My dear Amanda: While it's true I'm probably older than you, I do not hold to the tenant that 'time heals all wounds.' In my humble, lonely-hearted, older-aged opinion, I've learned that 'love,' not 'time,' heals all wounds. I say, 'Good riddance' to the floozy chaser and good luck with the love thing. Way before your time, Amanda, a very wise man wrote, 'All You Need Is Love,' and I still firmly believe that."

I really thought that this question and answer would elicit a response from Ana about 'love' and things of that nature, in her daily email to me. It didn't. Her email read:

"My dear Noah: I've finally decided where I'm going to vacation this year. But it won't be in Utah. Not that I don't love your beautiful state, but I want to see more of God's glorious creation and experience the width and depth of this exciting world. Always your friend, Ana."

"Always your friend, Ana." Friend? Doesn't she know I want to jump her bones? How can she not read between the lines and diagnose my feelings? I need a better plan . . . I need something . . . anything. Then my trusty inner voice calms me down and says, "Noah, Noah, Noah" (weird, because Noah's not really my name, but anyway, it continues): "You don't always need a plan. Sometimes you just need to breathe, trust, let go, and see what happens."

∞∞∞

I end up the day at the Moab Brewery. A comfortable place, but with too many tourists nowadays. I usually have a Black Raven Stout to start with and finish with. It's a dark, heavy, trouble-laden, intelligent brew—just like me. That's why I like it. I used to know several of the bartenders here, but they keep changing with the seasons, so I don't try to remember their names any longer-- except for the pretty ones. I usually remember their names: Susan, Doris, Danelle, Casey, etc., etc. But no Ana, never an Ana . . . that's what I'm afraid of—never an Ana.

So now I only stare down at my black, foamy brew and wish it would talk back to me. It doesn't. I guess I'm lucky in that it only takes one drink to get me drunk. The trouble is, I can't remember if it's the 13th or 14th.

∞∞∞

"Noah: I've tried coffee, tea, and expresso, but nothing seems to help me. I'm just not a morning person. I'm grumpy and grouchy until after lunch, then it's like I have a new personality and I'm friendly and funny and fun to be around. Do you have any advice for me to make it through the mornings? Signed, Grouchy."

"Dear Grouchy: I'm going to pass this along to my editor, maybe he can help you. I, too, am not a morning person or a night person. There are a few minutes in the afternoon where I'm decent and that's about it. Sorry."

"Noah: I don't understand women! Can you help? Signed, Frustrated."

"Frustrated: How old are you? It's taken you this long to figure out you don't understand women? Let me give you some advice to think about from someone who knows women inherently. First, you must understand this: Women are scientifically proven to be right even when they're wrong. A woman may be misinformed, misled, unclear, misguided, and even downright stupid . . . but she is never ever wrong! If the world was ruled by women, there would be no war . . . just a couple of nations not talking with each other. And, finally, Frustrated, when a woman says, 'Do whatever you want.' Do NOT do whatever you want. Please remember these rules, Frustrated. Your life will be a lot easier. Your friend, Noah."

This column did generate a response from Ana.

"My dear Noah: I didn't realize your complete and overwhelming expertise about women. I'm very impressed. I'm sure it's difficult for men to understand us at times—you know how men are. But for us, it's easy to understand men, we know what they want . . . don't we? And, unlike women, good men are found on every corner of the earth. But, unfortunately, the earth is round . . . isn't it?"

FOUR

"Dear Mr. Know-it-all, Noah. Explain this, if you can: How did Lee Harvey Oswald, who was known as a poor shot in the army, hit a moving target at several hundred yards away? And, why was the mysterious man on the grassy knoll never investigated? And how did the autopsy photographs of President Kennedy mysteriously disappear? And what happened to the President's brain, which was never seen again after the autopsy? Do you want to enlighten us all as to what you think about all this??? Signed, Very, very curious."

"Dear Mr. Curious: No."

"Noah: I heard through the grapevine that they're paying you over $100,000 to write these silly columns of yours. I think that's disgusting! You don't do anything, you don't research anything— all you do is spout off at the mouth and make fun of people. How can you justify taking all this money for doing nothing? Huh?? Signed, PO'd."

"Dear Pod: Get your facts first, then you can distort them as you please."

"Noah: A girl, who I thought was my best friend, stole my boyfriend. I'm so mad at them both I could just scream. I'm going to get them both back very soon. I just want you to tell all your readers that friends should be friends, not lying, cheating snakes. Because cheating snakes will be found out and we will pay you back—I promise. Can you please warn all your readers? Signed, Jilted and Mad!"

"Dear Jilted and Mad: I truly hope you get over this sad situation soon, but trust someone who has a lot more experience than you. Revenge is a poison meant for others, which we end up swallowing ourselves. An eye for an eye only ends up making the whole world blind."

"Noah: I have a friend who I know is doing something that's not exactly legal, but she also helps out some poor people and donates to Goodwill. That's good, isn't it? I mean, it's not really all that bad if she does some good, is it? Signed, Anonymous."

"Dear Anonymous: It doesn't matter how much lipstick you put on a pig—it's still a pig."

"Noah: What happens if you paint your teeth white with nail polish? Signed, Suzanne."

"Suzanne: Very interesting question. Weird, but interesting. Check with your dentist for an accurate answer and let me know what he says. Sure would save a bunch of brushing wouldn't it?"

Once again I'm off on my weekend hike. This time I'm hiking down the Escalante River Gorge. Since very few people have ever heard of it, I'm quite certain I'll be alone. This hike follows the Escalante River as it winds its way through the canyon country. Most of the time there's room to hike beside the river itself; however, sometimes the canyon walls converge directly into the river and one must wade through the knee-deep water for several minutes to find shore again. I don't mind this; keeps the riff-raff out anyway.

Today, I walk along the banks looking at the cottonwoods and quaking aspen, until I'm forced to wade into the water for a bit, then back onto the bank. In and out of the water; this is the main reason tourists never come here—plus, its way out of the way. After a couple of hours, I tire of this in and out so I stop and eat some snacks I've brought with me: an orange, some raisins, peanut butter crackers, and cheese doodles. After some reflection about life and Ana, and Ana and life, I turn around and start back down the river on the same trail I just came in on. After my first river walk I climb back up the bank, into the same footprints I'd just left several minutes earlier, except there are cat tracks on my footprints. More specifically, mountain lion tracks.

This cat's prints are on top of my footprints. I don't get too scared . . . after all, I have a Swiss Army knife with me. Might have been a coincidence anyway. I go back into the stream again and when I come back on the bank, the cat's tracks are again on top of my old tracks—it's been following me! For the next six times I go in the water and come out, the mountain lion's tracks are on top of my footprints. It's not only following me, but it's also stalking me.

I get my Swiss Army knife out of my pocket and mistakenly open the corkscrew first. Dang, where's that blade? I finally get the blade open and the 2 ½" weapon makes me feel much better—not safer, just better. Same scenario all the way back to the trailhead: Each time I get out of the water I see the cat's tracks on top of my old prints. This crazy cat has followed me down the river for over two hours, and yet I never saw it or heard it.

When I finally get into my car and lock the doors—just in case—only then do I breathe comfortably. And only then do I realize that since I saw that first cat track, I haven't thought of Ana at all. Fear can do that. This is one day when I realize that going out like this is good, but coming home is better.

☾☾☾

It's a long drive back to Moab and it gives me time to think about things. About mountain lions, Ana, my life, my dreams, Ana, my work, and ultimately—Ana. What am I going to do about her? What can I do? So many questions: Does she have long hair? Black hair? How old is she? And the most dreadful question of all, is she married? I don't think I'd really care exactly what she looked like, well, within reason. If she was six feet tall and weighed 367 pounds it might take some getting used to. But it's the allure of Ana, the dream of her, the fantasy, the illusion, the delusion—yes, all of that. And what can I do about it? Hike the canyons and mountains of southeastern Utah and answer questions and comments in my column from the good people of Salt Lake City. And once a day, read my precious email from Ana . . . dear, sweet Ana.

"Noah: I'm a very successful businessman here in SLC. I have a college degree and a master's degree, I make an excellent salary, and have a very good future with my firm. My girlfriend is beautiful, smart, and successful as well. I have it all. Why, then, am I unhappy? You're sort of smart—some of the time—can you answer this question for me: Why am I unhappy? Signed, Discouraged."

"Discouraged: No one is in charge of your happiness but you. Nothing I can say will change anything. However, I will tell you not to measure yourself by what you have accomplished, but by what you should have accomplished with your abilities. And, Discouraged, what I've found in my years of experience is that most people are as happy as they make their minds up to be. And so can you. Good luck."

"Noah: I like to sit around and listen to music. My mom says I'm lazy and that I'm wasting my time. What do you say? Signed, Curt."

"Curt: This is what I have to say: Time you enjoy wasting is not wasted time. But . . . I'm not your mom. Always listen to your mom, Curt. Always."

"Noah: I'm single and have a low-paying job. I like my job, it just doesn't pay much. All my girlfriends have relationships and seem happy. It's not that I'm unhappy, but I don't have a boyfriend. I can't afford to have my hair done every week or my nails done each weekend. Some of my friends have had boob jobs and one girl even had a butt implant. I can't do any of that stuff! I need some help! Signed, Plain Jane."

"Dear Ms. Jane: I sincerely doubt you're as plain as you think you are. I think it's your friends who have the problem. They're the ones who think they have to do things to themselves to be more attractive . . . right? Don't worry about them, Jane. I've always found that a SMILE is an inexpensive way to improve your looks. Try that, Jane; smile more, fret less-- I'll bet it works. Your friend, Noah."

"Noah: My son still lives at home and works part-time as an Uber driver. What can I do? He's thirty-three years old, he's still fairly young . . . right? What do you think? Signed, A concerned Mom."

"Mom: I read this quote once, which I think applies to your son: 'You are only young once but you can be immature forever!' Don't let forever last forever."

"Okay, Mr. Know-It-All: Which came first, the chicken or the egg? Signed, Stumped."

"Dear, Stumped: Genesis 1: 20-22

"Noah: Is it weird that my dog likes to watch me pee? Signed, Eileen."

"Eileen: It is the fate of glass to break."

"Noah: There's one thing I don't understand: How can one candidate get more votes than another candidate yet still lose the election? I mean, I know about the Electoral College and all, but I just don't understand how this is possible. Can you help? Signed, Confused."

"Confused: I can definitely explain this to you, but I can't comprehend it for you."

"Noah: Just why should we believe anything you say in the paper? We don't know anything about you, except that you used to be a sports writer—that doesn't make you smart. Why should anyone listen to you? For all we know, you could be a serial killer. Are you? Signed, Walter."

"My good friend, Walter: You don't have to believe anything I write. That's up to you, Walter. As for being a serial killer—no, I'm not. As Mark Twain once said, 'I've never killed a man, but I've read many an obituary with a great deal of satisfaction.'"

"Noah: Me and my friends like to have fun, but we're not crazy. My girlfriend thinks we're crazy—I think she's crazy. All we do is have fun. I bet my buddy that he wouldn't lick the floor of a school bus for $20. Guess what? He licked it! And one time we drove my pickup truck around town with a fake casket in the back (that we made) and we all sat on the casket and drank beer as we rode around. It was great! Tell her we're just having fun. Signed, Jimbo."

"Jimbo: Aliens are probably riding by earth and telling their children to lock their doors."

Another day, another column, and I finally get to wait for Ana's email. I could go out and play tennis, or play golf, or have a Black Raven Stout at Moab Brewery, or even cut my toenails. But instead, I sit here and stare at the computer screen waiting on a message from someone I don't even know. I'm pitiful. I'm going to stop this insanity. What's the point? I'll never meet Ana. It's all a dream. Child's play. I'm done. Do you hear me little voice in my head? I'm done!

Little voice in my head: "Never argue with someone who believes their own lies."

FIVE

"Noah: You seem pretty smart. Where did you go to college? Signed, Sigmund."

"You are correct, Sigmund, I did go to college. However, I didn't learn a thing but it was my own fault. I had a double major in Psychology and Reverse Psychology."

"Noah: Sometimes you make no sense whatsoever, then sometimes you make good sense. It's hard to tell with you—exactly how old are you?" Signed, Curious Jane."

"Dear Ms. Jane: To answer your question, I'm not young enough to know everything, but I am old enough to know that just because I can doesn't mean that I should."

"Noah: I'm sick to death of all these stupid taxes we have to pay. Sometimes I think our government exists just to tax us, and I'm sick of it. Do other states and countries have taxes like we do? Signed, Fed Up."

"Mr. Fed Up: I have certain rules I live by. My first rule is I don't believe anything the government tells me . . . Nothing! If we have high taxes it's because they want us to have high taxes—they voted it in—it's their decision. I personally don't think our country is as great as we used to be. We should be and we can be, but we've got to make changes, starting with all these stale representatives we have in Salt Lake City and Washington. A lot them have been there for fifteen, twenty, and twenty-five years! Are things getting better? No! So let's get rid of them and elect some new people. How about that, Fed Up? If it's important to us, we'll find a way. If not, we'll find an excuse and keep sending the same old, tired people back to tax us again and again. In the end, Fed Up, we tried, we cared, and sometimes that is enough. Thanks for writing."

~~~

This was a trying day with the column. I usually don't get too worked up with the questions and answers, but I went a little overboard today. I'm really looking forward to a quick stop at Moab Brewery, then reading my daily email from Ana. I'm lucky to find a corner seat at the bar so I can blend in and not have to talk to any of the tourists. It's not that I mind them, most of them are nice. It's just that they ask the same four or five questions all the time and I'm sick of answering them.

"How long have you lived here?"

"Does it get lonely here in the winter?"

"Did you know Edward Abbey?"

"Do you get a lot of snow here?"

"Are you married?" I hate this one the most.

So I sit here and try not to make eye contact with anyone except the new bartender, who seems like a nice enough guy. Across the way on the other side of the room is a table of four women who are sipping glasses of wine. The woman who is facing in my direction keeps looking over here, but at this distance, and my poor eyesight, I'm not sure if she's looking at me or at someone else near me. But every time in look in her direction, she's looking back at me.

I only meant to have one drink this evening—after all, Ana is waiting on me-- but since the woman is still looking over here, I order a second brew. Midway through my second pint, the group of women all get up and start for the exit. All except the one who has been looking at me all evening. She starts walking over towards me and smiling at the same time. Now I know she's definitely looking at me—and she looks pretty good, or is the Black Raven Stout clouding my judgment?

She walks up to me and says, "Hi, do you mind if I sit down?"

I have no idea who she is, but what the heck, so I say, "Yeah, sure, can I get you something to drink?"

"No, my friends over there are waiting for me. I just wanted to ask if you'd be interested in a timeshare we have available? It's a great location on the north end of town with a view of the river. I can get a great deal on it. Would you like to go take a look at it?"

I'm trying to figure out if she's asking me to go take a look at this timeshare—or go take a look at her. I guess I took too long to decide, so she said, "We'd love to show it to you."

I'm thinking of a thousand different responses, but finally say to myself, "Kindness is in my power even when fondness is not." So, I reply, "No, I'm very happy where I am. Thanks, anyway."

She smiles and leaves a business card on the table and says, "Well, if you change your mind, please give me a call."

Ana? Where are you? Come save me, please! I leave my half-full glass of Black Raven Stout on the table and head to my lonely home.

"Noah, I think it's time in our relationship that I volunteer some personal information- if you're interested. You may not be, but I think you are. Anyway, if not, you can stop reading now.

"Where to start? I am a college graduate, from a state college you are familiar with, with a degree in a field you would probably think is superfluous. I work at a challenging job—sometimes interesting, sometimes boring, and sometimes fun. I live in a small house which I adore. I have many hobbies and interests and things that keep me busy—including corresponding with you. And finally, in answer to a question you've asked, or hinted at, several times-- I'm not married. I was married, but that was a while back. I hope all this information quenches your curiosity. Your friend, and now confidant, Ana."

This is what I want to write back to Ana: "Exactly what have you told me, Ana? You went to college—but where, I don't know. You have a challenging job—but what kind of job, I don't know. You live in a small house, where? I don't know. You have many hobbies—what they are, I don't know. But you have been married—wow—you actually told me something! I can't believe it."

Instead, this is what I actually wrote back, "Ana, thanks for all the valuable information; I truly appreciate it. I have, indeed, been wondering about all those things (and more). I'm glad you cleared up a lot of unanswered questions. And you were married at one time. My, isn't that interesting? Thanks again, your friend, Noah."

"Grow a set and demand some answers, Noah!" Shut up, little voice in my head. What do you know? And, at least call me by my real name!"

ᴄᴏᴄ

"Dear, Noah: I have been retired about four years now. Each year it seems as though my children and grandchildren see me less and less. I understand that. Kids have other priorities in life than sitting around with an old person. My problem is that since I retired I don't have much to look forward to anymore. There's got to be more to life than watching Good Morning America every day, isn't there? Please tell me there is. Signed, Lonely Linda."

"My dear Ms. Linda: There is. You are never too old to set another goal or dream a new dream. I learned this from grandfather, Linda. He said, "You don't have to live forever, you just have to live.""

"Noah: My co-workers are a bunch of insensitive, nosy, and mean people. It's hard making it through each day listening to them complain, gripe, and not work. I know they don't like me because I don't join in their lunchtime griping sessions. Have you had any experiences like this? If so, how did you handle it? Signed, Fed Up!"

"Dear Fed Up: We probably all have experienced this to some degree. My only advice is to tell you that what other people think of you is none of your business. Fed Up, when people treat you like they don't care, believe them—and move on."

"Noah: Isn't there a law about having dogs on leashes? I'm sick of seeing dogs running around the neighborhood with no leash. Can you call somebody about this? It's dangerous! Signed, Kevin."

"Kevin: Here's what I found out. Exercise is totally unnecessary. It's overrated. And vitamins—forget 'em. If you want to live a long life, choose the right parents! And most of all, don't die too early. Hope this helps with your dilemma, Kevin."

"Noah: How many people actually live here in Utah? Signed, Lance."

"Lance: You know buddy, since you emailed this question in, it means you have some sort of device. Which means you have some form of Google. Which means you could just ask Google that question and you'd know the answer in about four seconds. But I'll be glad to answer the question for you of 'How many people actually live here in Utah?' Answer: All of them."

"Noah: I think I need to start exercising. Do you exercise? Can you recommend a good place to start a good exercise program? Signed, Chubby."

"My dearest, Chubby: Unfortunately, I cannot recommend a good place to exercise, since I don't exercise at all. I should, I know, and so should you. My hapless heart says chocolate and beer, but my jeans say, 'For the love of God, man, eat a salad!'"

"Noah: I really don't care about how much money I have in the bank, but I do care about all those less fortunate than me. I think all the people with a lot of money should share their wealth and not be so snobby about it. What do you think about all the wealthy people out there hoarding their money? Do you want to be like that? Signed, Andrea."

"I see your point, Andrea. Some people get so rich they lose all respect for humanity. That's how rich I want to be."

"Noah: Why does my screen say 'www.bangbros.com' after my son leaves, even though he tells me he is doing homework? Every night during the school year my son tells me he's doing homework on the family computer. Once in a while I come down to review but the screen comes up 'www.bangbros.com' and it's a girl. Is this a homework site? It tells me to give a password each time but I don't know it. Help, please! Signed, A concerned Mom."

"Dear Concerned Mom: Sounds like he is indeed doing some homework. Probably trying to learn some valuable life information about human inception and procreation (or recreation)."

Today's work is done, today's pint or two from the Brewery has been consumed, the appropriate number of people have been pissed off, so now it's time for me to see if my elusory and illusory friend, Ana, has left me any messages. Of course, she has,

"Noah, Noah, Noah. Maybe it's time we moved forward with our relationship and volunteered some personal information from ourselves. What do you think? I'll start. How old are you, Noah? Secondly, I never read in your columns about any close friends. Do you have friends or do you like the solitude you find in the desert? Can you honestly answer these questions for me, my friend?"

I thought about my reply for a long time. Should I be honest with Ana and answer her questions, or should I be just like her and continue to be coy and mysterious?

"Ana, Ana, Ana . . . I like saying your name, it's hypnotic. I'm glad you asked those questions because I've been wondering the same things about you. It's time we started being honest with other, so here are my answers. About my age, today I am the oldest I've ever been in my life—and the youngest that I ever will be for the rest of my life. And, the answer to your other question: If you like solitude then you're never alone."

Now, all I can do is wait until tomorrow to hear her reply. Will she be upset with me for avoiding her questions, or will she answer them herself? I can hardly wait.

SIX

After I eat a bowl of chicken vegetable soup and take a shower, I hear my computer ding with a message. I don't usually get messages this time of night—the paper sends me all my emails in the mornings. When I click on I find another message from Ana—highly unusual—she's already sent me my one daily email.

"My sweet friend, Noah (or whatever your name is). You enjoy being mysterious with me, don't you? I've opened up my life with you and I would simply ask for you to do the same with me . . . or, I could just leave you alone, if you prefer. Let me know. Your hopeful friend, Ana."

Well, well, well . . . isn't this a nice predicament I've gotten myself into. I'm sitting here staring at the keyboard wondering what—if anything—I should tell her. But I have to say something—I don't want her to get mad at me and stop writing. What would I do then??

"My dearest, Ana: I truly think we are the same age. We think alike, we act alike, we like the same things, we must be cosmically linked—don't you think? I will volunteer this about my life: I've found that it is far better to be alone than to be in bad company. I truly hope we can remain close, Ana. The cost of not following your heart is spending the rest of your life wishing you had. Always your friend, Noah."

Should I have written that "following your heart . . .?" I hope that doesn't scare her off. Thirty minutes, one hour, then an hour and a half—no more messages from her. Dang! On to bed and think and dream of Ana—or the thoughts of what I think Ana might be like. Boy, this is confusing.

"Noah: I've been reading your column for several months now and I just don't think you take things seriously enough. The world is in terrible shape: poverty, famine, wars—it's horrible. Our country is out of control, young people don't have a clue, and you—YOU just act like it's all one big joke. You are so immature, Noah—how old are you, thirteen? Signed, Disgusted."

"Disgusted: No, I'm not being immature, I'm having fun. You should try it."

———

"Noah: I've been dating my girlfriend now for over four years. She's starting to put some pressure on me to either get married or break it off. I don't want to lose her, but I don't think I'm ready for marriage yet. I love her, but I just want to make sure I'm 100% ready. This makes sense, doesn't it? Signed, Moses (not my real name)"

"Moses: I sort of thought that might not be your name. But anyway, Moses, I've always found that if we wait until we're ready, we'll be waiting for the rest of our lives."

———

"Noah: My boyfriend has been lying to me about everything. His job, his education, his friends—everything. He's just so cute, but how in the world can I have a relationship with someone who cannot be honest with me? What a gigantic waste of time this has been. Signed, Emma."

"Emma, Emma, Emma: You can't. Honesty is a very expensive gift; don't expect it from cheap people. And trust me, Emma, it wasn't a waste of time if you learned something."

———

"Noah: You don't sound like you're married. I've got a good friend I could introduce you to, if you're interested. Wouldn't you like to be married to a beautiful girl? Signed, Lucy."

"Dear, Lucy: Everybody has their own thoughts on marriage. Here's the way I see it: Marriage is like flies on a screen door. Those that are in want out; and those that are out want in. And that's my answer."

"Dear Noah: It's my first time writing to you and I feel a little awkward about it. But I need some advice from someone who is unbiased in my situation. I'm a divorced thirty-seven-year-old woman who has been dating the same guy for nearly a year now. He is also divorced but neither of us has any children. Here's my dilemma . . . my boyfriend acts a little weird sometimes when I question him about things. Also, he'll go off for several days but not tell me where he's been. Then he'll borrow money from me when he actually makes more than I do. And sometimes he gets these strange phone calls, which he always dismisses as wrong numbers. Things just seem a little weird, but he's such a good guy. What are your thoughts, Noah? And please be honest. Signed, Perplexed."

"My dear, Perplexed: Regarding your boyfriend, it is okay to be a little weird. But it is NOT okay to be an idiot. My advice to you is to follow your heart, but take your brain with you."

"Noah: Are there any autographs of Jesus Christ? I know there are autographs of Babe Ruth, John Lennon, and George Washington. But are there any of Jesus Christ that are either on eBay or in people's houses? Signed, James."

"James: I've researched this question extensively and found that anything is possible if you don't know what you're talking about. Let me know when the bidding starts."

"Noah: I have a sensitive issue I'm struggling with. As you know, they outlawed bigamy here in Utah a long time ago. However, I know a guy who has married two different women. He seems to be happy and so do they, though I don't understand how. Should I simply ignore this and let it go? What are your thoughts on bigamy and with this guy in particular? Signed, Very Concerned."

"Very Concerned: I thought about this guy that you described, and here's my conclusion: Bigamy is having one wife too many. In his case, so is monogamy."

Another day, another Black Raven Stout, or two, another night of anticipation from Ana. I go out to my back patio and sit in a rocker and watch the sun cast a shimmering glow across the La Sal Mountains as I wonder what Ana might be doing right now. What does one do in North Carolina? Do they have mountain ranges like the La Sals that soar over fourteen thousand feet high? Do they have vast areas of wilderness in which to lose your way or your soul? Do they have canyons and trails to wind away from your troubles and cares-- and maybe even your life if you're not careful? Maybe, maybe not, but it does have Ana, which is much more than this desolate scrubland of red rocks and sand can say.

Finally, the computer alerts me to an email. I was watching a hawk sitting in an old cottonwood tree as he was watching a rabbit run from bush to bush out beyond the property. Wonder who'll win that battle? Yes, the email is from Ana.

"My dearest Noah, or Larry, or Jerry, or Allen, or whatever your real name might be. How are you? I like your reply to the question of bigamy—I'm proud of you. I was sitting on my front porch this evening wondering what you might be doing. Wondering if you have the redbuds, the crepe myrtles, and the long-leaf pines to gaze it. What does one gaze at in the desert? Is there anything there? Noah, I must be honest with you. I've found myself thinking about you more each week and wondering if you're thinking about me. Are you? I might change my policy and answer more than one email a day if you care to write more than one a day. You certainly don't have to and I don't want you to feel as though you must. But, if you do, I'll answer you back.

"Good night, my friend. We are friends aren't we? Nameless and faceless friends? I tried going back in your paper's history to see if they ever published a picture of you before—I couldn't find one.

Maybe I'll try the Moab high school annuals—you did go to high school in Moab, didn't you? Always, Ana."

"Ana, my lovely . . . I'm assuming you're lovely. I know you are—you must be. Where do I start? Yes, please write more than once a day—I'd love it. No, I did not attend high school here in Moab. I thought you knew I only moved down here a few years ago to get out of Salt Lake City. Or, are you just testing me? In answer to your other question about what I gaze at in the desert—there is nothing here to gaze at. Only things that will hurt you—prickly pear cactus to stick you, quicksand to drown you, rattlesnakes to bite you, red rock ledges to cut your legs, canyons to kill you if you fall, poisonous plants to make you sick, and old lecherous men to lust after you—it's a dangerous place, my dear!

"Your other question, yes, of course, I think about you. Even though I don't know what you look like, or how old you are, at least I know your name—Ana. What a beautiful name. That is your real name, isn't it, Ana? Eternally, Noah."

Less than ten minutes after I sent this email to her, Ana writes back:

"My eternal, Noah. I'm so glad you like my name, just as I like yours. Even if your true name ends up being Jon or Mark or Matt or Scott, I think I'll always call you Noah—is that okay? Your desert sounds like a dangerous place to live. I hope you're careful out there. I'm not sure a city girl like me should ever visit such a wild and lecherous area. Thanks for warning me! If you're interested, you can always look back at my old high school annuals to see what I looked like back in the old days—only if you're interested. Unlike you and your secretive ways, I'll be honest and tell you that I did, indeed, go to high school here in North Carolina. So look me up! Sweet dreams, Ana."

She's playing with me! That's good . . . isn't it? Look up her old high school annuals in North Carolina? No town mentioned, no year mentioned, not even her name mentioned . . . yeah, I'll look her up. But she's playing with me—I like that.

☾☾☾

"Noah: I'm a fifty-four-year-old man who is sick of being fat and out of shape. I joined a gym and went every day for two weeks, then quit. Next, I went on a diet for a month, and all I lost was thirty days. I'm disgusted, depressed, fat, and at wits end. I don't think my body can withstand what it would take to get in shape. What do I do? Signed, Eric."

"Eric: Wow! That's quite a saga and I feel your pain. In my humble, out-of-shape, opinion, your body can withstand almost anything. It's your mind that you have to convince. Good luck, buddy."

"Noah: I'm writing to complain about all the potholes on our streets. It's disgusting! Why can't they do a better job? We pay a lot of money in taxes for good schools and roads, but our roads are terrible. I'm mad about this. What the Sam Hill is the problem? Signed, Georg."

"Georg: I have three questions for you: What is a 'Sam Hill?' Does your name not have an 'e' at the end of it? And, most importantly, Georg, for every minute you're angry, you lose sixty seconds of happiness. Is that what you want?"

"Noah: I'm the chairman of the local 'Save the Earth' committee here in the greater Salt Lake Region. I wanted to see if we could get you on board with our clean roads program. We want people to stop throwing their garbage out the windows of their cars. Our roadways are filthy. We need to leave a better planet for our children and grandchildren. We hope you'll join our group and publicize our efforts. You do agree that saving the Earth is important, don't you? Signed, Abbey."

"Abbey: I'm in full agreement with you! Yes, save the Earth! It's the only planet with beer and wine."

"Noah: I'm a high school senior and I've been accepted to Southern Utah University when I graduate. I'm proud of that, but a lot of my classmates who are going to Utah State, Brigham Young University, and the University of Utah are acting like they're now better than me because my school isn't as big as theirs. I think they're snobby about it and I don't want to compete in their petty comparisons. Why are people like that? Signed, Ruthie."

"Dear, Ruthie: Unfortunately, you will always find people like that throughout your life. Comparing their lives to yours, their car to yours, their husband to yours, their clothes to yours, on and on and on it will go. Just remember this, Ruthie, a flower does not think of competing against the flower next to it. It just blooms. Bloom, Ruthie!"

"Noah: Keep up the good work! I like you. Whatever you're doing to be so successful, keep doing it. Signed, Doris."

"Doris: Thank you for one of the most intelligent letters I've ever received. My basic key to success is playing the hand I was dealt like it was the hand I wanted. Thanks again, Doris."

"Noah: I wanted to take the time to write and say how happy I am that I live here in Utah and not to the west of here with those crazy people in California. Can you believe them? I think we should get down on our knees and pray we're not over there to the west in that crazy place. Do you agree? Signed, Blessed"

"Blessed: It seems like you're totally ignoring our crazy friends to the west of us in Nevada—I think people still live there, but I'm not sure. However, I did meet this girl from California once who was so ugly, when she was a kid playing in her sandbox, the cat kept trying to cover her up."

"Noah: I was bitten by a turtle when I was a young lad, so can I still drink orange juice? Signed, Billy."

"Billy: Glad you wrote. No! If you drink orange juice now it will activate the turtle venom in your veins and send you into a coma. Didn't anyone ever tell you this before?"

"Noah: My girlfriend is pregnant and we didn't have sex. How could this have happened? Signed, Jerry."

"Oh, Jerry boy, the pipes, the pipes are calling . . . No, seriously, Jerry. Last time you two went to a movie together, did you drink out of the same Pepsi cup?"

"Noah: I need help. I'm training for a bodybuilding championship and I'm on a strict diet. Is an egg a fruit or a vegetable—I really need to know? Thanks, Jeff."

"Jeff: Glad you asked that question; it's been a point of debate for years. Don't believe everyone! I've always found that it's easier to fool people than to convince them that they have been fooled. So, yes, you are correct, Jeff."

"Noah: I understand the right turn on red thing, I really do. But if there's nothing coming, why can't we also turn left on red? And go straight on red? I mean, if nothing's coming, we're just sitting there wasting gas, right? Signed Lonnie."

"Lonnie: The more I thought about your idea, the more I thought back to what my grandfather taught me as a young boy. He said, 'Noah, when nothing goes right . . . go left!' The best advice I've ever received."

"Noah: I am so disappointed with kids today. It seems they're all on the wrong track. They don't respect anything, they don't take responsibility for anything, and they don't seem to care about anything. It's truly pitiful and makes me sick to my stomach. Signed, Franklin."

"Franklin: You know what makes me sick to my stomach? When I hear grown people say that kids have changed. Kids haven't changed. Kids don't know anything about anything. We've changed as adults. We demand less of kids. We make their lives easier instead of preparing them for what life is truly about. We're the ones that have changed."

SEVEN

From: Ana

"Noah, I have some more personal questions to ask you and I hope you'll be truthful and answer them, okay? Are those questions in your column from your readers actually real or do you make that stuff up? Only curious. Next, have you ever been married? (Honestly?) Do you plan on living in Moab the rest of your life? Do you enjoy our long-distance relationship? Are you currently seeing any young (or old) ladies there in Moab? (Again, be honest) And finally, Have you ever visited North Carolina? If so, where?

"I'm anxiously waiting for your reply to all my questions. And, Noah, remember this: When in doubt, tell the truth. Always your friend, Ana."

So, Ana wants ME to tell her the truth about stuff when she's never told me anything. So, why shouldn't I tell her the truth? Am I ashamed of myself? Do I have something to hide? No . . . it's the point of the whole thing. She tells me nothing and she expects me to tell her everything. Okay, here are my choices: Keep being evasive and risk losing contact with Ana, or answer her questions and open up the possibility of a deeper relationship with Ana. Hmm . . .

"Ana, my dear, of course I'll answer your questions and, as always, I'll be 100% honest with you. I could never lie to you—I thought you knew that.

"First response, yes, the questions you see in the column are indeed from my readers. I could never make up some of that stuff. In fact, their questions are usually better than my answers, but they are all as I received them—except that I'll take out some cuss words every now and then.

"As I've told you before, NO, I have never been married, nor have I been engaged; however, I did date one lady pretty regularly one summer a few years back. We enjoyed each other's company and had a great time together, but she moved back to San Diego where she came from. I heard she married a stockbroker and lives in a great big house, with new cars, and is a member of a fancy country club. I hope she's very happy back in San Diego with her stockbroker. Certainly not the same life she had here with a columnist . . . not by a long shot.

"Do I plan on living in Moab forever? Quite honestly, I've never thought about it. It's nice here, but it's nice lots of places. It's probably nice in North Carolina, or New York, or anywhere you settle and put down roots.

"Yes, I very much enjoy our long-distance relationship—as opposed to no relationship at all. However, if I had a choice of a long-distance relationship or a more intimate one, well . . .

"Your next question . . . Yes, I see young and old ladies every day. Moab is full of them. But I bet you meant to ask 'Am I dating any young or old women?' didn't you? No, I'm not.

"And, yes, I have visited North Carolina in the past. I hiked part of the Appalachian Trail for a few days. I visited Andy Griffith's hometown once and drove to the Outer Banks that same trip just so I could say I've been there. But to be honest, it was a long time ago and I don't remember much of the trip, except that it was a long drive from Mayberry to Nag's Head.

"There, 100% honest and accurate answers to your questions. Now, will you do me the same courtesy if I ask you five or six questions?

Your totally honest and forthright friend, Noah."

Five minutes after I sent this message to Ana, she wrote me back:

"Oh, Noah, I'm so sorry. I forgot to ask my most important question—what is your REAL name?"

"Ana, Ana, Ana . . . my dear sweet girl. Not until you answer my questions first!"

"But you haven't asked me any questions?"

"They're coming. And I KNOW that you will be just as honest as I've been . . . won't you?"

Silence, silence, silence. Then seventeen minutes later, this answer from her:

"Noah, the best way to find out if you trust somebody is to trust them."

"Ana, my dear sweet, Ana . . . What is your real name?

How old are you?

Are you dating anyone right now?

What town do you live in?

What sort of job do you have?

What color is your hair?

Where did you go to college? (I know you did go, so I don't have to ask that.)

"You asked me seven questions, and now I've asked you seven questions. I answered all your questions honestly, now let's see if you'll answer my questions honestly. But, I'm sure you will. Won't you, my dear?

"Waiting anxiously, Noah"

Ana did not answer my questions immediately; I guess she's thinking of appropriate responses—or, how to twist the truth around and still be vague about everything. Anyway, back to work,

"Noah: my neighbor is the most ignorant man I've ever met. We end up arguing nearly every day, about everything. If I like something, he doesn't like it; if he does like something, it's always something I despise. I'm sick and tired of arguing with this crazy man. Do you have any suggestions? Signed, the real McCoy."

"The real McCoy? Excellent. Through my many years of experience, Mr. McCoy, I've found that it is impossible to defeat an ignorant man in an argument. My advice—quit trying."

"Noah: My husband wants us to take a vacation to France this year. I like France and I think it would be great, but I also think we need to wait until we're in better financial shape. Last year he wanted us to go on a cruise, but I talked him out of that. It would've been fun but we needed to save some money for a new refrigerator. He keeps bringing up all these ideas and it's getting harder and harder for me to explain to him why we need to wait. Any suggestions? Signed Amy?"

"Amy: I'm going to give you MY opinion. Now remember, I'm not a financial analyst, a financial planner or your banker—I'm only a lonely columnist answering some questions. So here is exactly what I think: Amy, I don't know how old you and your husband are, but it really doesn't matter. It's time to start living! Never allow waiting to become a habit. Live your dreams and take risks. Life is happening now! Fall in love with your life, Amy."

"Noah: I'm a single, middle-aged man here in Salt Lake City. I haven't been married and have worked very hard, I've saved and invested well, and I'm looking forward to retiring soon. I've talked with several financial consultants about how much money I need to retire comfortably, and they all have varying answers. What sort of wealth do YOU think I need to retire with and be financially secure and happy? Signed, Luke."

"Luke: That's an interesting question. In my opinion, you'll never be wealthy enough until you have something money can't buy."

"Noah: Last year sometime you ran an article about things drunk people can't say. Can you reprint that? Signed, DL."

"DL: I remember that article well, but I can't take credit for it. It was sent to me by my friend Dwight, and I don't think he'd mind if I reprinted it. Here it is—top phrases drunk men absolutely cannot say:

1. No thanks, I'm married.
2. Nope, no more booze for me!
3. Sorry, but you're not really my type.
4. No thanks, I'm not hungry.
5. I'm not interested in fighting you.
6. Thank you, but I won't make any attempt to dance. I have no coordination and would hate to look like a fool.
7. I must be going home now as I have to work in the morning."

"Noah: I don't understand Daylight Savings Time. We aren't saving any daylight—it doesn't make any sense! All we're doing is changing the clocks. Who are we trying to fool, anyway? There's nothing scientific about it. Do you have a logical explanation for this? Signed, Mike."

"Mike: Very good point. I did some research on this subject and have found that the universe contains protons, neurons, electrons, and morons. Hope this clears it up."

"Noah: I've met a girl that I really like. I think she likes me too but sometimes it's hard for me to tell. All I know is that I can't stop thinking about her. How do I know if it's 'love' or not and how can I be sure if I'm 'in love?' You're sort of old, what do you have to say? Signed, Scott."

"Scott, Thanks for the confidence in my opinion. You can read all sorts of books and watch all kinds of talk shows on TV about love, but in my opinion, LOVE is a lot like a backache. It doesn't show up on X-rays but you darn sure know it's there. Trust me, Scott . . . you'll know."

"Noah: I just spent a weekend with my family in another city. I was so glad to get home and back to my friends that I smiled all the way home. Is there something wrong with me to want to be with friends more than I want to be with my family? Does that make me a bad person? Signed, Charlie."

"Dear Charlie: Here's how I look at that issue: You're stuck with family, you have no choice with them. Oh, yes, you love them (most of the time) and you care for them, but you have no choice in the matter. Whereas, friendship is a wondrous thing. The love of friendship is often stronger than the love of brotherhood or sisterhood. There is a chord of tenderness and appreciation binding those who are friends, which is lovely beyond words to express it. Friendship must have good soil in which to take root, for care and cultivation. The good seed of friendship is love and affection. The soil must be constantly stirred by kind acts, words of appreciation and affection, and mutual admiration. So, I totally understand your situation. My conclusion is that you're totally normal, Charlie—at least about friends and family."

EIGHT

I make a quick trip to the grocery store for essential items: toothpaste, doughnuts, deodorant, coffee, Diet Mountain Dews, Hershey chocolate bars, and vitamins. Then a quick stop at the brewery, just to check on things, before going home to wait on my email response from Ana. C'mon, c'mon, c'mon . . . I hate slow internet service. Finally . . . junk mail, junk mail, junk mail, bill, bill, junk mail, ED advertisement, more junk mail, then I see it—a response from Ana!

"Noah, my dear sweet, Noah: I'm glad we are finally being entirely honest with each other—it's about time, don't you think? So, that being said, here are the answers to the seven questions you asked me:

"What is my real name? It's Ana, of course. That's what you know me by, that's the name you admittedly like, and so, that is my real name for all my correspondence with you. Even if my name were Mary or Dorothy or Pat or Gail—would you ever feel comfortable with any of those? No! You know me as Ana and so, my friend, Ana it is!

"Second question: How old am I? Noah, I truly feel like you and I are the same age. We think alike, we act alike, we see things similarly—therefore, we MUST be the same age. Don't you agree? If I was a great deal older, or younger, than you, it would be very evident for either of us to see in our writings. No, I am very confident we are exactly the same age. So, however old you are, is exactly how old I am. Don't you agree?

"Third question: Am I dating anyone right now? No. Unless going for coffee is considered a date. Or maybe a movie, or a quiet dinner every once in a while . . . but dating? No.

"Fourth question: What town do I live in? I don't really live in a town, Noah. I live outside any city boundary lines, out in the country—where a girl belongs.

"Fifth question: What type of job do I have? I have a job that pays me adequately, but not too much. A job that is very demanding, yet satisfying. More specifically, a job that is part of a government agency.

"Sixth question: What color is my hair? Really? You're interested in that? Are you referring to before my college years or after my college years? Before or after my latest visit to the hairdresser? Honestly, Noah, it changes subtly with the seasons. As in lighter in the summer and darker in the winter. You know how women are about their hair.

"Seventh and last question: Where did I go to college? I'll be more than happy to give you that information, Noah, but you probably want it to go to my college annuals and see my picture don't you? However, the last name I had in college is not the last name I have now—so that wouldn't help you too much. But still, I'm proud to tell you that I attended College of the Ozarks.

"Seven questions asked and seven questions answered! I hope this satisfies your curiosity, Noah, and maybe now we can really start getting serious and personal in our communications—okay?

"Always your friend, Ana"

I read this email from Ana about a dozen times. Then I went to the refrigerator, got a beer, and read it another dozen times—or twenty—I lost count. She really only told me a few things I didn't know. Mostly, she was vague and extremely non-committal with her answers. However, there is one thing of which I'm certain, after reading this email forty or fifty times . . . I'm in love with Ana (or whatever her name is).

The next morning I read the email four more times before starting work, just to make sure I didn't miss anything. Concentrating on my work might be difficult today,

"Noah: I read your advice and comments to the person who questioned you about visiting his family versus visiting his friends. I liked that. But, still, you must visit your family and do the right thing. It might not be the most pleasant thing we do, but it must be done—am I right? Signed, Becky."

"Thanks for writing, Becky. I received several emails about that particular answer. I will clarify my opinion a bit now for all of you still wondering about this: I believe Santa Claus has the right idea. Visit people once a year."

"Noah: I read your column a while back about country music and enjoyed it. I wanted to tell you my three favorite country songs and see if you also like them:
'I Ain't Never Gone to Bed With an Ugly Woman, But I Woke Up With a Few.'

'If the Phone Don't Ring, You'll Know It's Me,' and

'She Took My Ring and Gave Me the Finger.'

What do you think about these, Noah? Signed, Willie."

"Willie: Well old boy, I do like all those songs . . . I get misty thinking about them. However, my personal favorite is that old popular tune, 'She's Looking Better With Every Beer.' That one always brings tears to my eyes."

"Noah: I can't seem to find the right guy. Every time I think I find some nice man, it turns out he's just not the one. I guess I have high standards, but I don't want to settle for someone who's not perfect for me. Do you think I'm being too picky? I just don't think I could be happy by lowering my standards. Signed, Robin."

"Robin: I wish I knew more about you and your history before making a judgment call, but I don't, so I'll give you the only answer that makes sense to me. The truth is that none of us are easy to date, deal with, or please all the time. We have our vices, attitudes, and way of doing things that make us who we are.

"You won't like everything about somebody; it's impossible! This is life and it isn't about finding the perfect person, it isn't about living some fairy tale. It's about finding something you're willing to work for, with somebody who's willing to work with you. That simple. Find someone who has a heart for you and never stop fighting for them. Good luck, Robin."

"Noah: if you could give advice to your younger self, what would it be? Signed, Marcus."

"Marcus: I would tell myself to learn the rules better so I'd know how to break them properly."

"Noah: I really don't know if you're religious or not. Sometimes you make fun of religion and sometimes you're serious. So, I'm not going to ask you that question. However, I would like to know what you think about all these people who value material possessions and seem to put materialism ahead of spirituality in their lives. What are your thoughts on this? Signed, James."

"St. James: I honestly don't think God's quarrel is with material goods, but rather with material gods."

"Noah: My wife, who is fifty-seven years old, wants to go back to college and finish her degree. It would take almost three years to do that. It's crazy; she would be sixty years old when she finishes. She doesn't need to work, and I make more than enough for us to live comfortably. Don't you think this is a crazy idea of hers? Signed, Watson."

"Watson: Here's what I think . . . once you stop learning, you start dying. Life is too short, Watson, not to enjoy it. I hope she has a blast in college and learns a great deal as well. You should try it too."

"Noah: I try my best to be healthy. I exercise daily, I watch what I eat, I take vitamins every day, and I monitor my heart rate. Why, then, am I sick all the time? I'm not old, I'm not fat, I'm not out of shape, but I keep a cold nearly year round, I always catch whatever is going around the office, and I'm sick of being sick. My doctor says I'm doing all the right things, so I'm looking for any help you can offer. Signed, Sick and Tired."

"Sick and Tired: Wow, that's quite a story. If your doctor says you're doing all the right things, I don't see where I could add anything. The only thing I'm sure of, from personal experience, is that I know life expectancy would grow by leaps and bounds if green vegetables smelled as good as bacon."

"Noah: If you could have only one, wealth or smarts, which would you take? Signed, Jack."

"Jack: Dang, that's a hard one. But I honestly feel that unless you love someone, neither one of these makes any sense."

"Noah: I'm an older guy who is retired, but still trying to live, if you know what I mean. I meet with some old friends from work once or twice a week at a coffee shop and we sit around and tell old stories and talk. It started out as fun, but I've been dreading it lately because a lot of these guys just have no common sense whatsoever. I usually end up leaving there mad at everything and in a bad mood because of the crazy things these guys talk about. I don't think I'm the smartest guy in our group, but I sure am glad the Lord blessed me with the gift of common sense. That's all I have to say. Goodbye. Signed, Norwood."

"Norwood: Common sense is not a gift, it's a punishment because you have to deal with everyone who doesn't have it. Good luck."

NINE

Time for me to take a walk in the desert and free up my mind. I'm going to take the White Rim Loop, which is a challenging eleven-mile trail through the Canyonlands with multiple elevation rises and some minor climbing involved. I've been on part of it, but I've never done the entire loop. But I am now—hopefully. The trail starts off pretty level and soon the tiny path through the dirt gives way to sandstone, where the trail is once again only marked by little stone cairns.

This gives me time to think and evaluate my feelings towards Ana and what I need to do; or more precisely, what can I do? What do I know? She has hair color that may, or may not, change with the seasons. She might be my age—maybe. She lives in the country—but what country or state? She's not married and I don't think she's dating anyone unless you count going for coffee, or a movie, or dinner actually dating someone. Hmm.

She went to The College of the Ozarks, which I'd never heard of, but Google said was in Missouri. Now how did a girl who vacations in Utah and lives in North Carolina end up at college in Missouri? Interesting. I found that the College of the Ozarks is also referred to as "Hard Work University," because all students are required to have full-time jobs when they attend. Also, it's FREE! That's why the students have to be employed full-time. Very interesting. The school gets them jobs in the community or the school itself and they work to pay for their tuition, room and board.

What else do I know about Ana? Let's see . . . Nothing! Whoops, where am I here? I'd better concentrate a little more on the trail. I'd walked towards the White Rim drop-off without paying attention. It's only about 800' straight down. Back on the trail now, the terrain is becoming a little more challenging with some climbing and elevation changes. This is not a touristy area, so I'm quite alone out here. After about ninety minutes I find a nice boulder and sit down to have some water and eat a few almonds and raisins, and think . . . about Ana.

The weather out here in the high desert can, and does, change quickly. It can be sunny and warm, then change to overcast and cool rather quickly, so you have to bring a coat even though you might not need it. I think nowhere on earth is there the type of scenery you find here in southeastern Utah: It's the perfect mix of ruggedness, awesome beauty, pristine canyons, clear streams, and brilliantly colored sandstone formations. An easy place to get lost if you're not careful. I have to concentrate more on the trail and less on Ana now that I'm in the back of beyond.

Scrub oak trees cling to some overhangs, little patches of prickly pear cactus spring from the cracks in the sandstone, and pinyon pines cluster in some of the overhangs, where rainwater drips occasionally. Tromp, tromp, tromp . . . up and down I go. Sometimes climbing, sometimes breathing heavily and sometimes lost in thought—it's all good. Surprisingly, I make my way back to the trailhead before it started getting dark, which is a good thing. I shake the dust off my shoes, my pants, and my shirt; drink the rest of my water; eat a Hershey's bar I'd forgotten about (which was mostly melted); and start back to civilization. Or, as one forgotten southwestern scribe aptly defined it—syphilization.

The Moab Brewery makes everything feel better, except I can barely get in the door. All the bar seats are taken and no tables are open either. Oh, well, I have a couple of bottles of some stagnant, stale watery Rocky Mountain brews back in my refrigerator. They'll do while I check my emails from Ana. I fire up the computer and take a quick shower to wash off the last of the dust from the trail. When I sit down I find two emails from my dream girl. The first:

"Dearest, Noah, I hope you're well today. Since I haven't heard from you all day, I'm assuming you're either very busy or maybe mad at me for the answers I gave to your questions. Let me know which.

"Always your friend, Ana."

And the second email:

"Okay, Noah, I'm getting a little worried why you haven't emailed back. Are you okay? Are you out on a date? Did your computer crash? Or, have you forgotten about me?

"Brokenhearted, Ana"

Well, well, well . . . Ana is worried about me, and she's brokenhearted. Isn't that interesting? Maybe she's starting to like me as much as I like her. It's possible.

"Dear Brokenhearted Ana, I am so sorry I worried you. I was indeed very busy today with a long, arduous, dangerous, exhausting trek into the unknown desert." (It's okay to exaggerate a little when speaking with women—they expect us men to do that). "I just returned and read your messages. Certainly, you must know that I could never be mad at you. Your answers to my questions were truly appreciated and treasured." (And it's also okay to tell little, white lies to women—they expect that as well).

"It's nice to know that you are a little concerned with my welfare and that you were thinking of me—that was very nice. Maybe on your next vacation, you could plan a trip to Moab and I could show you all the interesting, dangerous, magnificent, incredible sites here in my hometown. What do you think?

"Your personal guide, Noah"

Fifteen minutes after I sent this message, I get the following response from Ana:

"Dearest Noah, thank you so much for the offer of a personal guide through the dangerous Canyonlands. However, I'm not certain I could afford your rates—I'm sure you're very expensive—nor could I physically endure the dangerous, ominous hikes you take into the depths of the unknown. You are indeed a brave man, my dear Noah. You are, in fact, my hero! Yours truly, Ana."

Okay, now she's just messing with me. I bet she's sitting there in North Carolina somewhere, sipping some sweet tea and eating bar-b-cue, just giggling over her email to me. Oh, Ana . . . how am I going to sleep tonight?

I didn't sleep much. However, the work emails don't care if I'm rested or not. They continue:

"Noah: If you knew the world was going to end tomorrow, what would you do tonight? Signed, Addison."

"Addison, my friend: If I was smart enough to know that the world would end tomorrow, I'd take all the money I had and go to Las Vegas and bet it all on Red-14. Because if I'm smart enough to know the world will end, certainly I'll be smart enough to know where the roulette wheel will stop. I'll be famously rich for one night. I'll give half my winnings to charity and I'll party like there's no tomorrow with the other half . . . because there will be no tomorrow—right?"

"Noah: I'm a Mormon. Why don't you like Mormons? You're always making fun of us in an abstract sort of way. What have we done to draw your ire? Signed, Sinclair."

"Sinclair: I've never said I don't like Mormons. I have questioned some things I don't understand, but I never said I didn't like them. There are simply some things that seem strange to me about the Mormon faith. I'm sure you have some perfectly reasonable explanations for these questions:

- You teach Jesus had three wives and children while He was on Earth. Where did that come from?
- There is not a single map in the Book of Mormon. Is it because there is not a single scrap of archaeological evidence to support your claims? Just curious.
- Your prophet, Joseph Smith, prophesied that the second coming of Jesus would happen in 1891. What happened?
- Joseph Smith also taught that there were inhabitants on the moon. Are there?
- Brigham Young taught there were inhabitants on the sun. What say you?

- There is not one shred of evidence, or proof, that any of the places in the Book of Mormon, or any of the tribes or battles told of, ever existed on earth—none! There is no archaeological proof to support anything in the Book of Mormon.

"These are just some of the questions I have, Sinclair. I'll be interested to hear back from you. Your friend, Noah."

⌇

"Noah: Is the reason you don't have your picture in the paper because you are ugly? Signed, Lucas."

"Lucas: Exactly right. In fact, when I was born, I was so ugly that the doctor slapped my mother!"

⌇

"Noah: I've read your column for quite a while now. As you know, I'm a city councilman here in Salt Lake City. It seems to me that every time you criticize the city or something we've accomplished, that you're thinking of me. I find that insulting. I'm just trying to do the best I can for the people in Salt Lake City. Signed, The Honorable City Councilman, Addison M. Buckholtz."

"Dear Mr. Honorable City Councilman, Addison M. Buckholtz: If I got a dollar for every time I thought about you, I'd start thinking about you."

⌇

"Noah: I was supposed to get a raise and a promotion and it didn't happen. Instead, they gave the promotion to some jerk who is now going to be my boss. All I wanted to say, that can be printed, is that life isn't fair! Can I say that? Signed Mad Hatter."

"Mad Hatter: That's a good one! You know what, Mr. Mad Hatter, life is never fair, and perhaps it is a good thing for most of us that it is not."

"Noah: You seem to be a fairly smart guy, maybe. What is your answer to this question—would you rather be rich and alone, or poor with a good family and friends? Signed, Marquis."

"Marquis: I thought a lot about this issue and I asked myself this question: Noah, who do you think is more content—a man with ten million dollars or a man with six children? What do you think, Marquis? I think the man with six children is more content because the man with ten million dollars is always wanting one more."

"Noah: I read your column about country song titles recently and it was pretty good. I'm not a country music fan but now I might be interested to check out a few of those tunes. Are the lyrics as good as the titles? Signed, Curtis."

"Curtis: I'm certainly no expert on country songs, but one song has always stuck with me in times of female troubles. It's an old Willie Nelson tune that goes like this:

> The postman delivered a 'past due' bill notice
>
> The alarm clock rang two hours late
>
> The garbage man left all the trash on the sidewalk
>
> And the hinges fell off the gate
>
> And this morning at breakfast I spilled all the coffee
>
> And I opened the door on my knee
>
> But the last thing I needed the first thing this morning
>
> Was to have you walk out on me."

TEN

Ana smiled to herself as she sent off her last email to Noah. She was happy with her replies to him, but she was also insecure, a bit intimidated, intrigued, excited, and guilt-ridden. Guilt-ridden? Yes, because she knows exactly who Noah is, what he looks like, how old he is, and generally everything else about him. How? Because she too lives in Moab, Utah, a fairly small town of about five thousand people, where most of the regulars know each other—or at least they know of each other. She knows him. He makes her smile; it's as if he knows a joke she doesn't know. She thinks she's in love with him.

Part of what Ana told Noah was true. She is originally from Lumberton, North Carolina, where she grew up in a poor county to poor parents. Her father was a white man from a family of tobacco farmers who barely stayed above the poverty line. Her mother was a Lumbee Indian who worked in a textile mill her entire life for minimum wage. Ana's parentage gave her a wonderfully tanned-looking skin tone, but not much else. Her father drank himself to an early death when Ana was in high school, and her mother basically ignored her. Ana was born when her mother was only fourteen years old, so her mother was still a child herself and didn't understand, or even much care, how to raise a kid.

Ana never had anything but was always bright and inquisitive. College was a dream to her. Her family had no money and neither did she. Then, through the high school guidance counselor staff, she heard of College of the Ozarks, which was tuition free—if you worked full-time to pay for everything. Ana thought that was the best deal she'd ever heard of. She applied, was accepted, and went off to Missouri for her education. She never went back to North Carolina, except for the funeral of her mother and grandfather.

Upon graduating from college, she found a job with the National Park Service and worked in several parks around the country. She loved it. It gave her the chance to see the country, which she would have never had without this job. She eventually ended up at Canyonlands National Park near Moab. She works in several administrative capacities at the park and even fills in at the park entrance station, which is where she first came into contact with Noah. On one of Noah's frequent hiking trips to the park, he had forgotten his park pass and the ranger on duty called Ana to see if she had a record of Noah in the computer. She walked over to the ranger station from her office and met Noah for the first time as she handed him his duplicate pass. For her, it was close to "love" at first sight. Especially when she took the time to engage in a short two or three-minute conversation with him.

From his park pass questionnaire she could see where he lived and what his job was. That's where it all started. Soon she began writing him at his newspaper and asking questions, always using a fake name. It had only been recently that she introduced herself as Ana to him. She had seen him around Moab at the pharmacy and grocery stores, and several times at the Moab Brewery, but had never been brave enough to try and introduce herself to him. After all, what would someone like him see in someone like her? So, she began playing the game with him. Why? Because she couldn't help herself. What did she think would ever happen with these games she was playing? Nothing, because she wasn't good enough for someone like Noah.

ᏭᏭᏭ

"Noah: I forget where you said you were from. Are you from Utah or somewhere else? Sometimes it seems like you don't understand our customs and ways here in our home state. Signed, Cole."

"Cole: Homey, I'm not really from Utah; I'm from Salt Lake City, which we all know is not part of Utah. It's a weird subdivision that has its own laws and customs. But I'm learning about the real Utah very quickly. I'll bet you didn't know, Cole, that we have laws on our books here that says it is illegal to fish while on horseback. Did you know that? Also, it is illegal to hunt whales in Utah. How about that Cole? And finally, just to show you how much I do know about our state, I found out that it is also illegal to walk down the street carrying a paper bag containing a violin. So, you be careful out there, Cole. You've been warned."

─────

"Noah: Why can't we get our trash picked up on time? It's frustrating to see our trash cans sit out front a day or two and nobody come empty them. What's wrong with these people? Are they stupid? Signed, Garland."

"Garland, Garland, Garland: I have two answers for you: First, worry less-- live more. And, Garland, my friend, don't be yourself today-- be someone nicer."

─────

"Noah: I'm trying to lose some weight but I just can't seem to be successful at it. I don't know what to do. Do you have any tips that would help me? What do you do to lose a few extra pounds? Please help! Signed, Laura."

"Laura: My dear, losing weight is harder than understanding quantum physics. I truly believe that. However, when I've tried everything else and have failed, I then write my stomach a letter: 'Dear stomach, YOU'RE BORED, not hungry. So, shut up!' I'm waiting for the reply . . . I'll let you know if it works, Laura."

─────

"Noah: I'm in a quandary. I know my co-worker is cheating the company and making false claims. I've seen him do it. It's illegal what he's doing and I should turn him in for it. But I'm afraid I might be classified as a 'tattletale' or 'informer.' I don't know what to do. The easiest thing would just be to forget it and let it go. What do you think? Signed, Nancy."

"Nancy: Don't do what is easier, do what is right."

─────

"Noah: From what I see, you make everyone mad. You make the liberals mad, the conservatives mad, the Christians mad, the Mormons absolutely hate you. How do you handle all this? Signed, Elizabeth."

"Elizabeth: Oh, my . . . I am aware of this phenomenon, Elizabeth, but I can't make everyone happy. I'm not bacon."

"Noah: I know this might sound a little crazy, but I need to know. Can an aardvark bark? Please answer. Signed, Ernie."

"Ernie: I will answer your question. An aardvark can bark, but only when the moon is full. So, when you hear an aardvark barking you can rest assured the moon is full, my friend. Hope this helps."

"Noah: I've heard that in West Virginia they are allowed to marry their cousins and even sisters. Is that true?" Signed, Morris."

"Morris: That is not true. Our friends in West Virginia have often been maligned for no apparent reason. By the way, do you know what they call a pretty woman in West Virginia? A tourist."

"Noah: I read on the internet that being right-handed means you will live, on average, nine years longer than if you were left-handed. Is that true? If so, why would anyone want to be left-handed? Signed, Omar."

"Dear Omar: If you read it on the internet, then it has to be true. As to why they would want to be left-handed, that's simple: It's a known fact that left-handed people get the prettier girls. Strange but true, Omar."

"Noah: Please settle an argument between me and my friends. Who's the best of all time: Madonna, Michael Jackson, or Justin Beiber? Signed, Kali."

"Kali: Okay, here's my answer . . ."

ELEVEN

It's not too crowded tonight at the brewery; I might even get a hamburger and fries. This time of year brings out all the mountain bikers to the Moab area because of all the slickrock trails around. I don't really mind them too much; at least they're better than all the off-road hucksters out there tearing up the wilderness. I see a few pretty women in here tonight, none by themselves. The table full of real estate women are here again; I move my chair around so I don't have to face them. It's odd, there always seems to be a lot of guys here by themselves—like me—but I never see a woman here by herself. I wonder why that is?

Anyway, I do order the Arches Burger and a Black Raven Stout as I sit here and think of what I'm going to say to Ana in my nightly email to her. There's something about Ana that I can't quite distinguish, but I know that it's driving me crazy. I'm going to try and find out where she lives in North Carolina and maybe even visit there on my vacation. How will I find that information? I have no clue. I did look back at the yearbooks for the College of the Ozarks for the years when I would've been a student there—since Ana said we were the same age. Only one girl in the senior class was named Ana—and I hope she's not my Ana. But since Ana is not her real name, I guess it's not her. I looked through all four classes and none of them struck me as my Ana.

What was I looking for? I don't know . . . I was hoping someone would jump off the page at me and I could say, "There she is! There's Ana." But it didn't happen. There were some pretty girls and some not so pretty girls—just like in any college yearbook. How long can I continue chasing this phantom dream of mine? Somehow, I have to convince Ana to give me more information about herself. How?

ᙅᙅᙅ

Back to work.

"Noah: Why are there so many mattress stores? And why are mattresses always on sale? Are they ever not on sale? And, finally, do you think this is a conspiracy to flood us with mattress companies? Signed, Holmes."

"Holmes: In answer to your questions about mattress stores, I don't know. I don't know. I don't know. And, yes, it is a conspiracy. I feel your pain. I often dream of a better world where chickens can cross the road without having their motives being questioned, and where anything is possible if you've got enough nerve. I'm sorry, Holmes . . . what was the question again?"

"Noah: I'm fairly old and I've witnessed a lot in my years on this Earth, but I've never seen the world in such bad shape as it is now. There are so many evil people out there that I don't know how they'll all be stopped. I'm very concerned! Who is going to stop all these crazy, evil people here in our country and in the rest of the world? Signed, Elaine."

"Elaine: Thanks for writing. I totally understand your concerns. But I firmly believe that the world will not be destroyed by those who do evil, but by those who watch and do nothing."

"Noah: There's this nice guy at work who I think is going to ask me out on a date. The problem is that he's not very good-looking. I know that sounds bad and makes me seem like a cruel person, but shouldn't we be attracted to someone we go out with? I mean, I like him, he's funny and interesting and smart, but I'm not sure I actually want to date him. I don't know what to tell him if asks me out. Any suggestions? Signed, Mae."

"Mae: Speaking from the perspective of a guy who is 'not very good-looking,' why don't you start with a 'yes' and see where that takes you."

"Noah: I'm a high school senior and trying to improve my grades for college. I have a complaint and a question: Why do we have to keep taking math? I mean, we all have smartphones that can answer any math question that ever comes up. So why do they make us learn this stuff? I mean who cares if Y x 5 = 2X? Signed, Max."

"Max: The entire issue here started at the beginning of time when Satan got mad and said, 'Put the alphabet in math!' Blame it on him."

"Noah: I wrote you a question last week and I think you were rude and not very nice to me. Do you ever apologize for things you write to people? Signed, Tina."

"Tina: Hello. I apologize for hurting your feelings, I didn't mean to. I'm sorry for what I said when I was hungry."

"Noah: I was coming home from school and saw a truck full of pigs that my mom said were on their way to be killed. Can't something be done about that? What's your advice? Signed, Rebecca."

"Rebecca: My dear, advice is what we ask for when we already know the answer but wish we didn't."

Noah: It seems to me nobody in our state or national government knows what the devil they're doing. Kids nowadays seem out of control, if not downright stupid. Both political parties are run by a bunch of jackasses, and the leaders of the other countries in the world are just as inept. What's happening to our world? How did it get this bad and why does everything in the world suck? Signed, Disgusted."

"Disgusted: Did you ever think about this . . . if the world didn't suck, we'd all fall off."

"Noah: Why are there so many dead squirrels and raccoons in the road? I know they can see us coming. Heck, if I tried to walk close to one of them, they'd take off in no time flat. Why do they let cars run over them? I don't understand. Signed, Melvin."

"Melvin: Don't believe everything you think. I feel pretty certain these poor critters did not want to be flattened by your SUV. However, you made one good point: When they see you 'walking' towards them, they instinctively run away. But, in their world and in their little brains, they have NEVER seen anything as big and fast as a car coming at them before. In nature there is nothing like your SUV—they don't understand it. Before they can figure out how fast it's coming, they're dead. Their life is not like a human's life. With us, life shrinks or expands in proportion to one's courage. Not with them, Melvin . . . courage usually means they die."

"Noah: My husband is as old-fashioned as they come. He never changes anything, except his underwear—maybe. Just kidding about that. But not kidding about him. He likes the same things now as he did twenty-eight years ago when we married. He likes the same foods, the same music, the same old movies, the same vacation spots—he never tries anything new. He's been driving the same kind of car ever since I've known him. When I complain, all he will say is that he's 'going with the flow.' Is there anything I can do to get him to try new things? Signed, Annie Lou."

"Annie Lou: In my humble opinion, only the wisest and stupidest of men never change. And I don't know your husband, but in my observations only dead fish go with the flow. Wish I could help."

"Noah: Can anything be done about these disgusting TV shows on the air now? I'm not happy at all with the filthy and vulgar talk I'm hearing every night. Also, I can't even listen to the radio without hearing swear words and the F-bomb all the time. Plus, it makes me truly unhappy to hear teenagers talking amongst themselves and the language they're using. Can anything be done, or are we all just going to be unhappy for the rest of our lives? Signed, Myrtle."

"Myrtle: Find something you enjoy and quit watching shows you don't like. It's important to make someone happy, and it's important to start with yourself."

TWELVE

Finally, I put my pajamas on (which consists of boxer shorts and a tee shirt from my trip to Las Vegas), poured myself an Iron Maiden, and waited for my nightly email from Ana. Turns out I didn't have to wait at all; the email was already waiting for me:

"Noah, my anonymous, impending, yet imminent friend, how are you? I find myself thinking about you more and wondering if you are thinking about me more than usual. So many questions I'd like to ask you, but maybe the time isn't right just now. I wish I knew what your hobbies are and what you do in your spare time, and what you enjoy, and . . . just everything. I have the strong feeling that we probably share a lot of the same passions in life. Anything you care to volunteer would be greatly appreciated.

Your inamorata, Ana"

I quickly Google "inamorata" and that it means "a sort of sweetheart." Ana considers me as her sweetheart? I could think of several other nouns to better identify what I think she is—or could be—but this is good. Isn't it? I answered her right away:

"My dear Ana, I am thrilled to be considered your inamorata. I looked that word up in my southeastern Utah booklet of seldom-used words and phrases and found that it actually means 'a person with whom you'd like to take a week's river trip with down the Colorado.' Yeah, I think I could work that in my schedule, Ana. Let me know when would be good for you. I'll supply the raft, the beer, the food, the sleeping bag, and the entertainment. You only need to supply you. Can't wait to hear back from you.

Excitedly yours, Noah"

Ten minutes later I heard from Ana: "Noah, I noticed that on the river trip you mentioned 'sleeping bag,' singular. Then immediately referenced 'entertainment.' I was wondering if the two were somehow intertwined or you had simply been careless in your use of nouns and verbs.

Anxiously, Ana"

I MADE himself wait ten minutes before answering—it was agonizing, but I waited. My answer: "Intertwined."

"Noah, Noah, Noah. Aren't you the bad boy? Inferring things like that to a good, old-fashioned, southern lady like myself. Should I bring a bathing suit on this trip or is skinny-dipping preferred?"

"My dearest Ana, I've often found that a wet bathing suit doesn't have time to dry properly on a raft trip. It's always much easier on the trip to dispense with anything that may hinder the ease of packing and unpacking—simpler is better. It's only for the good of the trip that I'm even suggesting this.

Very professionally yours, Noah"

"So, let me make sure I understand everything about this trip before I commit. You and I will raft down the Colorado together— just the two of us. We'll only have one sleeping bag. We won't need bathing suits because they may impede our progress, skinny-dipping is preferred, and you will provide beer and entertainment. Am I missing anything?"

"That pretty much nails it, Ana. When can you come?"

I sat up until nearly 2:00 am waiting on her reply . . . Nothing! But she didn't say "no" either. I've come to believe that very few things are indeed impossible.

Ana did not answer Noah's last email because she didn't know how to answer Noah's last email. How long can she continue her deception before it either gets too dangerous, or worse, not dangerous enough? Sometime in the future, near or far, she's going to have to divulge her secret and let Noah know that she is living in Moab, just like him. That she has been misleading him or lying to him all this time. What a tangled web we weave when first we practice to deceive. But as she feels guilty thinking about this old yarn, she also remembers and KNOWS that Noah would never be interested in her if they met in person. Living in cyberspace and anonymously is the only chance she'll ever have of a relationship with him.

She recently read a quote that described her situation pretty accurately: "Most people are other people. Their thoughts are someone else's opinions. Their lives a mimicry. Their passions a quotation. Be you!" How can I be me? I can't even tell him my name, yet I can't let him go. She knows that deep inside it takes courage to grow up and turn out to be who she really is. She also knows that she doesn't possess that courage at this point in her life. Living the dream is much more fun. And . . . is that bad?

I was taking the day off from my column and devoting it to two things: thinking about Ana and doing nothing. I was looking forward to each of them. I started the day at the Slickrock Café and had a cup of coffee as I dreamed of Ana. I added some cream and stared down at the steam rising from the cup as I spoke to it, saying, "Come here you big, beautiful cup of coffee and lie to me about how much Ana misses me and loves me." Coffee can do that.

After filling my head with dreams, I casually walked down the main street of Moab, passing all the tourist shops, sandwich shops, and jewelry stores and ignoring nearly everyone I passed. After a few blocks, I stopped in front of a government building and sat on the bench out front to rest and watch the tourists walk by. Unbeknownst to me, a meeting of national park rangers was just breaking up in the government building and they were all filing outside going to their pickup trucks (no locals drive cars in Moab— only pickups).

Ana (not her real name) was in this group of rangers. She was talking to a fellow ranger from Arches National Park as they walked along when she suddenly stopped and nearly fainted. Her fellow ranger didn't even notice and kept on walking. Ana saw me sitting on the bench by myself. I wasn't doing anything but sitting there and enjoying the day. She moved a couple of steps closer to get a better look at me but stayed behind me. Her heart was racing and her mind was urging her forward: "Go talk to him, tell him who you are, stop all this pretense." But she couldn't.

Soon, I rose and continued my wayward journey through town. Ana followed behind me for about two blocks, but when I went in an ice cream shop she kept on walking—walking on air in her case. She found her Canyonlands National Park pickup truck and sat inside waiting for me to come out of the ice cream shop. However, a fellow ranger walked by and asked her for a ride back to the park, so she abandoned her quest and left her heartstrings there on the streets of Moab, outside an ice cream shop, where the man of her dreams sat inside, completely and overwhelmingly unaware of her presence in this world.

THIRTEEN

"Noah: I just read that Princess Diana was actually alive hours before she died. Do you think this is true? Shouldn't it be investigated? Signed, Paul."

"Paul: Yes, you're exactly right. We need to get the National Enquirer to investigate exactly how someone could actually be alive hours before they died. I have their number, BR-549. I'll forward this to them. Thanks."

"Noah: Why can't we get a Major League Baseball team here? Salt Lake City is better than San Diego, and Cincinnati and Baltimore and ten times better than Texas, and they all have baseball teams. You need to start publicizing this and initiate the program to get it started. Can you do that? Signed, Bowie."

"Dear Bowie: Unfortunately, I do not feel the same as you do on this subject. Baseball is boring! Nobody watches it but old men, baseball doesn't have pretty cheerleaders, and there's never any action. What we need here in Salt Lake City is an NBA team. Basketball is fun and exciting and never boring. There's plenty of action and the NBA would wake this town up big time! Hold on a second, Bowie . . . I'm sorry, my assistant just informed me that we already have an NBA team here. Do you have any other questions?"

"Noah: I have a question: Shouldn't we look into the claims made by the basketball star Kyrie Irving about the world being flat? He should know; he flies all the time and he can see the Earth when he's flying. Plus, he went to Duke University—he's smart! I know it might sound ridiculous, but isn't it possible that all the scientists and politicians have been deceiving us all these years? I mean, it is possible—isn't it? Signed, Charles."

"Charles: Think! It's not illegal yet."

"Noah: Why can't the United States give money to all the poor people in our country instead of giving it to other countries? Can anyone explain this? We have veterans, old people, disabled people, all sorts of disadvantaged people here, yet we continue to give away our money to foreign countries. Why? Here's an example of what I'm talking about: Last year we gave

> Tanzania, $520 million;
>
> Ethiopia, $580 million;
>
> Nigeria, $625 million;
>
> Kenya, $625 million;
>
> Jordan, $676 million;
>
> Egypt, $1.56 billion;
>
> Iraq, $1.68 billion;
>
> Pakistan, $2.1 billion;
>
> Afghanistan, $2.33 billion; and
>
> Israel, $3.1 billion.

What's wrong with this picture, Noah? Am I missing something? Signed, Thoroughly Disgusted and Confused."

"Dear Sir: I agree."

"Noah: My wife and I were out to dinner last weekend and she said she saw you sitting at the bar with a woman. She's sure it was you, but she also said your date was not very attractive. Sorry, but that's what she said. Could this be true? Signed, Malcolm."

"Malcolm: It could very well be true. The last girl I dated was so ugly she went to the beauty parlor and stayed nine hours. And that was only for an estimate."

"Noah: It's Vernon again. I wrote to you a few weeks back to ask you about how many stars there were in the sky. You told me there were more stars in the heavens than there were grains of sand on every beach in the entire world. I have researched this thoroughly and I think you might be right. I didn't believe you at first, but as I said, you might be right. Thanks for not lying to me, Noah. I appreciate that—I might just love you as much as I do my morning coffee! Signed, Vernon."

"Vernon: You're welcome, and I love you more than coffee . . . but please don't make me prove it."

"Noah: I told my girlfriend that as soon as I graduate from college, I'm going to get a great job; buy us a big, fancy house and new sports cars; travel the world; write a best-selling book, and retire early. She laughed at me. I think it's possible—don't you? Signed, Mickey."

"Mickey: I think you can do anything, but not everything."

"Noah: I'm having trouble meeting the right guy. I'm pretty attractive, I have a good job, I have lots of girlfriends who all like me. I'm pretty active and like to have fun, but I can't seem to find the right guy. I mean, there are lots of guys interested in me—don't get me wrong; I'm pretty hot. But I feel like I'm unique and I should be able to attract a unique guy as well. What are your thoughts? Signed, Eloise."

"Eloise: I think you're exactly right. Always remember that you are unique. Just like everyone else in the world."

"Noah: I've found that as I'm progressing into middle age, my political views have changed somewhat. The way I look at the world seems to be at a different angle now. Have you experienced this? Signed, Roy Retrospective."

"Roy: You are not alone. Apparently, middle age is when broadness of the mind and narrowness of the waist change

---

"Noah: I'm a tired, worn out, fairly young man who feels like he's old and extremely frustrated with the 'rat race.' I'm too young to retire and too old to start over. I feel trapped by this infernal rat race of work and life. How do you win at this, Noah? Can you win? Signed, Brent."

"Brent: I'm sorry, dude. And, I know you probably know this already but, the trouble with the 'rat race' is that even if you win, you're still a rat."

☙☙☙

This last question and answer dampened my spirits so bad I got in my car and drove out of town a few miles and just started walking in the desert. You can do that here in southeastern Utah. All people need a place to get away to, a place to hide and not think, a place to let your mind wander where it will go . . . where it will go.

FOURTEEN

I was going to sit at my computer and write Ana a long email, but I had two emails from her before I could write anything.

"My dear Noah, it's hard for me to believe that a worldly, successful man like yourself is sitting at home doing nothing every night. Please be honest and tell me the truth, what do you do each evening? Especially your weekend evenings? Are there any young ladies you're escorting around the wilds of southeastern Utah?"

Then her second email, "I have been reading about Moab and the surrounding areas. You have two National Parks close to you, Arches and Canyonlands. Have you visited them often? If so, which do like better? As always, your Ana."

My Ana? I wish she was mine, then I wouldn't have to sit around here by myself and . . . well, you catch my drift. I think it's good she's reading about Utah and the national parks here. Maybe I can convince her to come and visit. But first I'll answer her questions.

"Ana, my lovely, you know I'm only waiting on you and would never dream of spending time with any other woman. What do I have to do to pry you out of North Carolina? I know if you give Utah a chance, you'll love it. Let's compare our two states:

North Carolina: overcrowded beaches, low mountains, sprawling cities bumping into each other, rednecks, and worst of all, Ana, you're bordered by South Carolina!

Utah: wide open spaces, clean air, majestic fourteen thousand-foot, snow-covered mountains, the Great Salt Lake, unrivaled majestic canyons, the Colorado River, national parks that will fill your mind with unimaginable visions, and finally, my dear, Me—I'm here in Utah.

Now when you look at both states with an unbiased eye, it's an easy decision, is it not?

Your tour guide in waiting. Faithfully, Noah"

As Ana read these emails from Noah she felt a twinge of guilt emanate from within her soul. She typed back seven different responses to him, but none of them said what she really wanted to say, which was, "Noah, I think I love you, please forgive me for misleading you. Please come and take me away and make me yours forever." Before she met Noah, she felt as though she was dying since the day she was born. Now, she could see a future, she could see happiness . . . if only she could figure out a way to get Noah into her life.

She was glad to read that he was not involved with another woman. If, indeed, he was telling her the truth. There was only one way to find out. She would have to use a few days of her vacation and actually spy on Noah this weekend and see if he was telling the truth or not. "Yes," she thought, "that's a great idea!" Sometimes, the devil in our head makes perfect sense to us.

So, she didn't answer Noah's last email that evening. She went outside her home and stared up at the starry night outside her home in Moab—the same sky that Noah would be staring at once he realized no further emails from Ana would come this night.

Canyonlands National Park was more remote and not as "touristy" as Arches National Park, so it was easier for Ana to be granted a few days off. Moab itself was rather small and almost all the places of interest were located on the main street through the middle of town. She decided she would first ride by his house and see if his car was there. If not, she would just casually stroll around town Saturday afternoon until she either saw his car or him walking the streets.

✆✆✆

I was looking forward to Saturday so I could maybe take a weekend hike or just take it easy and hang around the apartment and have a drink or two at the Moab Brewery. Plus, I was nearly out of food and other necessities so I needed to do some shopping. Like most men, I usually wait until I am completely out of something before I restock. So this morning, when I could barely get the last remnants of toothpaste out of the shriveled up tube, I knew I had to go to the store.

Ana drove by and saw Noah's car was not parked at his place. She immediately drove into town and parked at the public lot behind the Slickrock Café. She walked five blocks north, then crossed the street and walked seven blocks south. She didn't see his car or him. But being a national park ranger prepared you to be patient—and she was. She went into the Back of Beyond bookstore and ordered a hot chocolate from the café inside. She found a small table by the window and sat there sipping her drink while staring out the window. After two refills (which were not free), she abandoned that post and started walking down the street.

She next stopped at The Dairy Ranch, where she ordered a Mountain Dew and sat on a bench outside under a zelcova tree. She nursed the drink, making it last so long that the ice melted before she drank it all. She saw the entire population of Moab pass by, except one, the only one she cared about. Near the end of her watch there she realized she needed to find a bathroom fairly quickly. But she knew, SHE KNEW, if she went into a bathroom, that's when Noah would come by. So, she held it.

She couldn't really walk comfortably in her condition. But she could cross her legs a little tighter and loosen the belt on her jeans a notch—every little bit helped. After a few minutes, an older lady stopped in front of her, looked down at her, and asked, "Are you okay, honey?"

"Yes, ma'am, I'm fine." She wondered why this lady would even ask such a silly question.

"Okay . . . you know they have a bathroom inside, don't you?"

Ana was stunned and answered, "What do you mean?"

"Honey, I had three daughters of my own. I know when a girl has to pee."

Ana didn't answer. The woman patted her on the shoulder and said, "It'll be okay. Don't hurt yourself." Then she continued her walk down the street. Ana looked over her shoulder to make sure there was indeed a bathroom inside. There was. It was calling her name:

"Ana . . . Ana . . . c'mon girl."

Ana waited until there were no people in front of her, then she squirmed inside and fortunately found the bathroom unoccupied. Just as she knew what would happen, it happened. Noah rode by on his way to the market to buy toothpaste and other essentials. Isn't that the way life is sometimes?

Ana remembered that Noah had mentioned the Moab Brewery before, so she thought she'd ride out there and check out the parking lot before she gave up her quest for today. The brewery was on the southern edge of town, on the way to where Noah lived. Ana pulled in the parking lot, which was full, and took her time and rode around the lot twice before she was convinced Noah wasn't there. "Okay," she thought, "this was only one day. I'll keep trying."

"Toothpaste, deodorant, sugar, peanut butter, coffee—do I have coffee? Do I need more? Crap, I should've written this stuff down." It's not easy being a man in a grocery store. Your senses are screaming at you: Cookies! Beer! Snacks! But your brain is saying, "Slow down, big fella." It's hard to know what you really need versus what you really want. I settled for a little of both. On the drive back home, I decided to stop by the brewery for a quick one before I went to check my daily emails from Ana. If he'd just left that bag of doughnuts alone, he would have made it to the brewery just as Ana was pulling out, and she would've seen him. Doughnuts are a man's best and worst friend.

FIFTEEN

"Noah: My boss at work is not a good man. He's abusive to all who report to him. He screams and curses at us, then he takes all the credit when things turn out well. When he does annual reviews for us, we all get less than satisfactory comments. A lot of people just quit because they can't take it any longer. I can't afford to quit; frankly, I need the insurance and benefits too much. Can he not see how he treats his staff? Doesn't he see how bad he is? What's wrong with this man? Signed, Scared and Angry"

"Scared and Angry: I'm so sorry for you and the others who have to endure this type of behavior. Unfortunately, you're probably not the only ones with this story. I fear that there are bad men, like your boss, in all types of situations. From my experience, a man who is 'moderately' bad knows he is not very good—and might change. But a thoroughly bad man 'thinks' he is all right and will never change."

"Noah: My husband and I just got back from a two-week trip to England and it was amazing. The culture, the history, the universities, and the theaters—it almost overwhelmed us. All throughout history England had led the world in innovations and literature and music—it almost makes me want to move there. What do you think is England's greatest gift to the world? Signed, Dianne"

"Dianne: In my humble, non-biased opinion, I think Britain's greatest gift to the world is AMERICA!"

"Noah: I teach Sunday school for teenagers and love doing it. However, I'm not very happy when you talk about having a beer or two in your columns. I don't think it's a good influence on young people. What is it that leads you to think drinking a beer will better your life anyway? Signed, Meg."

"Meg: That's a good question. I certainly don't want to be a bad influence on teens—or anyone, for that matter. But I just don't think a beer or two, enjoyed by responsible adults, is harmful. In fact, I think beer makes you feel the way you ought to feel without beer."

"Noah: I've done some stupid things in the past but I'm trying to straighten out my personal life. There is such a fine line between winning and losing that it is hard for me to keep on the straight and narrow. I want to do good, but more accurately, I don't want to do bad. I'm tired of being a loser. Any words of wisdom from you? Signed, Gene."

"Gene: I have always found that the difference between winning and losing is most often not quitting. Good luck my friend."

"Noah: I have a friend who is just different. She dresses oddly, she says things that seem crazy, and at times she just doesn't fit in. I've tried being her friend for quite a while, but let me tell you, it's not easy with her. Do you have any advice for me to give her? Signed, Vicki."

"Dear Miss Vicki: If you're lucky enough to have a friend who is different . . . never change her."

"Noah: Sometimes my husband can be so immature. He still listens to music from when he was a teenager and will dance around the house acting crazy. He loves sports and will yell and scream at the TV over some ballgame he's watching. I love him, but I wish he'd grow up a little. Any advice? Signed, Prudence."

"Dear Prudence: (Did I just say that?) Anyway, I have to take your husband's side here. I would advise him, and you, to stay close to anything that makes you glad you're alive. Once you're grown up, Prudence, you can't come back."

"Noah: I cannot understand how to save some information to files on my computer. My word processing in Excel and Microsoft is all screwy. And I can never download information without increasing my googabytes, or something like that. I hate this crap! Aren't there any computers for old people? Signed, Red."

"Red: I feel your pain. I miss the days when everything worked with just an 'on' and 'off' switch."

"Noah: I know a guy who is always carrying around a Bible and saying prayers in front of groups of people. But, I also know he cusses sometimes and talks behind people's backs. He also lies to some of the girls about stuff he does. I know he's a hypocrite, but it just bothers me. Signed, Joseph."

"Joseph: He sure sounds like a hypocrite . . . but aren't we all? A donkey carrying a pile of holy books is still a donkey."

"Noah: I want to know what you think about racism in America. Don't you think we should love all black and brown people? Signed, Tom."

"Tom: Okay, I'll tell you what I think—maybe you'll like it or maybe you won't, but here it is: I think to like an individual just because he's black or brown is just as insulting as to dislike him because he isn't white. Tom, you can't depend on your eyes when your imagination is out of focus."

"Noah: I don't know why you like to make everyone so mad. It's like you go out of your way to annoy people. Why can't you just try to make people happy every once in a while? Is that asking too much? Signed, Bill."

"Bill: If I wanted to make everyone happy, I'd stop telling the truth and start selling ice cream."

PART TWO

SIXTEEN

Ana made it back home a little disappointed but determined in her quest to actually learn more about Noah's personal life. She decided to write him another email—that always made her feel better.

"Noah, my dear, I read your email contrasting North Carolina and Utah. It seems rather one-sided, don't you think? However, you did make Utah sound very interesting. I might even want to visit there again and do some hiking in one of your national parks. Do you think I'd enjoy it and not get lost out there in the wilderness?

Ana"

Less than ten minutes later she received a reply from Noah:

"Ana, my lovely, you know I would never let you get lost in the wilderness. I would protect you from all the wild and dangerous animals, and be your human compass which leads you to green and fertile pastures in the oasis of life's pleasures. You have my word. Please come visit as soon as you can.

Anxiously, Noah."

Just reading this email made Ana blush slightly. No man had ever spoken to her as Noah has. Then she wondered if Noah actually knew who she was, would he still be speaking to her like this. Certainly not. Why does she keep playing this game? Why is she fooling herself? Why is she fooling Noah? Why is she hoping for the impossible? Why? Because she can't help it, and because impossible isn't a fact, it's an opinion.

She had another email from her boss at Canyonlands National Park:

"We need your help, please. Ranger Dula had appendicitis and just had an operation. Can you fill in tomorrow and lead the weekly hike through the White Rim Canyon? Thanks, see you in the morning."

Her boss knew she couldn't say no. She knew she couldn't say no. Her quest for Noah would have to wait a week or two. The White Rim hike is completely over slickrock with no markings whatsoever. An inexperienced hiker would probably get lost and never find his way out: This is why a ranger always guided the weekly hike into and through this remote region. Ana had done it several times and had almost become lost herself. About six or seven tourists would usually be on the hike. Once she led fifteen people on the hike, and a few times she only had two or three with her. There were no reservations, just whoever showed up and wanted to go was welcome.

Noah sent the last email to Ana and waited for a reply, which never came. The allure of Ana was now consuming him. Somehow, he had to find out where she lived in North Carolina and go there. He knew if he could somehow find her it would be a fairy tale ending—they would both live happily ever after—he was convinced of that. He finally gave up and sat out on his patio, looking at the stars, as he finished the last of his drink. It was always nice to dream about Ana . . . always.

When he woke in the morning he still had no email from Ana. He knew he couldn't sit around all day and stare at the computer screen, so he gathered his backpack and headed out for a hike. He'd been thinking of the White Rim Trail at Canyonlands National Park but had never had the nerve to try it by himself. Today he would—if he didn't chicken out.

When he arrived at the park headquarters, he found that a ranger was going to lead a hike through the White Rim today and anyone was invited. Perfect! Someone to lead him so he wouldn't get lost and die. He milled around the gift shop with four other women in their hiking gear, waiting on the ranger to come out and start the hike. Noah was a little concerned that these four middle-aged women were not in good enough shape to do this day-long hike, but they'd find out soon enough.

Ana finished her paperwork and walked out of the office to find four women eager and ready to go. She said, "Is everyone ready for a great adventure?"

"Yes, let's get started" answered the leader of the group.

"Does everyone have water and some food? It's going to be a long day?"

"Yes, ma'am. We're all good, but I'm not sure about the guy in the bathroom."

Ana asked, "What guy?"

"There's a guy who wants to go on the hike. He's not with us, but he seems ready to go."

Just as Ana started to ask another question, Noah walked out of the bathroom drying his hands on a paper towel. Ana was so stunned that she couldn't speak. All the other women were staring at Ana wondering if she was okay. Noah took a couple of steps towards her and asked, "Is it okay if I come along or is this hike for women only?"

Still, Ana didn't speak. She was almost afraid that if she spoke Noah would recognize her voice and her cover would be blown. Then she realized she had never actually spoken to Noah except through emails. "Yes, no, of course, you're welcome. Are you ready?"

"Yep," Noah answered, wondering if this stammering lady ranger was indeed the right person to lead them out into the wilderness and back.

Ana was in a fog. How did this happen? How did Noah get here? What was he doing here? She hadn't put on any makeup. She hadn't done anything to her hair. At least she did take a shower this morning. Think girl . . . think!

The group followed Ana up towards the first incline, with Noah settling in the rear to keep to himself as much as possible. None of the women were what he considered "pretty." The ranger woman wasn't really pretty, but she wasn't ugly either, and she wasn't plump like the other women. Oh, well, hopefully, she wouldn't get them lost or killed.

After a rather strenuous start to the hike, the trail settled into a more reasonable level, only a few minor ups and downs, as it wound itself into the depths of the unknown. After a couple of hours, Ana stopped in an area with a nice view of an overlook for everyone to take a water break and have a snack while they rested. All the women talked amongst themselves during the hike while Ana stayed well in front and Noah stayed well in the rear. But when the group stopped, everyone came together . . . introductions were necessary and forthcoming. Ana was dreading it.

The four women all introduced themselves. Noah tried to remember their first names, but he wasn't good at remembering names, so it was pointless. Then he introduced himself as "Noah." He had started doing this lately when around strangers because of his infatuation with Ana. Also, because he knew he'd probably never see these people again anyway—so what difference did it make?

When Ana heard him announce his name as Noah, she audibly gasped, then quickly covered it by coughing a couple of times. She wondered why he called himself Noah in front of these people. That's not his name! She knows his name . . . it's not Noah. She wonders, "Does he know me? Is that why he said his name is Noah? He must know me. What do I do now? How do I handle this?" As her mind is racing trying to answer these questions, one of the other women asks her what her name is.

She can't say Ana. And she can't think. She doesn't want to say her real name, just in case Noah is playing with her, so she quickly blurts out, "Just call me Ranger. That's what everyone else calls me . . . just Ranger."

The four women all say "Hello, Ranger."

Noah looks at them like they've all lost their minds, but gives a little smile as he also says, "Okay, nice to meet you, Ranger."

The four women start chatting among themselves again and Ana turns her back on all of them to pretend she's reading a map— hoping Noah doesn't ask any questions. He doesn't, he's too busy eating some M&M's and a granola bar. Ana exhales as she finally concludes Noah does not know her true identity. She finds it hard not to look back at him. She wants to look back at him. Why? Because now she is absolutely certain she is in love with him.

Ana leads on and the others follow her, certain that they could have never hiked this trail alone without getting lost. They stop a few more times for rest and snacks and to enjoy some views. Each time, Ana leaves them and pretends she's going up ahead to scout the trail. When in fact, she's only trying to stay away from Noah. She doesn't know what she should say to him or what she should not say to him. She's so confused that it's easier to stay away from him and not compromise herself. Plus, he seems to be making friends with the least plump of the other women.

Noah and this one woman did exchange some chocolate with each other, but that's about it. He wasn't interested in anything except the views, how much chocolate he had left, and when they would return. He really needed to check his emails to see if Ana had answered him. His phone did not have service out here in the middle of nowhere and he had convinced himself that Ana had emailed him. He also wondered why the ranger lady always left them when they stopped. That was odd behavior. Plus, she never actually made eye contact with him. She would never look at him directly. She always addressed the other women—never him. Maybe she didn't like men. Some women were like that. Some women had good reason to be like that. But it was still odd.

The hike had been everything Noah had hoped for: scenic views, breathtaking vistas, and not one other hiker on the trail the entire day. He was happy when they arrived back at the cars--he was tired. He shook hands with all the other women and they said their goodbyes as the ranger woman quickly walked away into the park headquarters. Noah sat there thinking about what he'd seen and what the sunset would probably look like out here in an hour or so. And, hoping the brewery wouldn't be too crowded when he got back to Moab.

Ana went straight back to her office and peeped through the blinds as Noah went to his car. Then, the little voice in her head started talking to her, "You should've told him who you are! Are you crazy, girl? What are you waiting for?" Then the devil inside her answered, "You know you're not good enough for him—don't you? You know he'll never be interested in someone like you. Forget him. Let it go. Quit dreaming and get back to reality you dumb girl." Fortunately, her good voice answered, "Shut up!"

Ana was still trembling a little as she watched Noah drive away. She was too excited, too hyped up, too everything to go straight home tonight. She knew Noah always went to the Moab Brewery, so she would have to go elsewhere to sit and unwind tonight. She would go to Main Street to the small Slickrock Café to unwind and think about what just happened.

SEVENTEEN

"Noah: Your paper said leaves and limbs would be picked up on certain dates around the city. Mine have not been picked up. Will you please notify the proper authorities and get this taken care of? Thank you, Marsha."

"Marsha: To give anything less than my best is to sacrifice my gift. Therefore, I WILL go directly to the editor of the leaf and limb department and demand that the leaves and limbs be picked up on time throughout the city. Always at your service, Noah."

"Noah: Every day when I read the paper and see all the crazy things people have done, it simply astounds me. Yesterday I read where a man and his wife withdrew over five thousand dollars from their savings account to buy lottery tickets because the husband had a dream he would win. Two days ago there was a story about two college guys who were arrested for impersonating police officers when they tried to search and frisk some college girls at a party. What is going on with people, Noah? Signed, Marianne."

"Marianne: We will never be able to understand why people do what they do. Most of us have some reasoning powers and we listen to that little voice in the back of our head that tells us not to do something. Others of us have a little voice that bets us five dollars we can't."

"Noah: I just had my 50th birthday. I don't feel that old, but some days are a challenge now. I wonder how other people adjust to the aging process and at what point they actually admit they are old. Forty? Fifty? Sixty? How do you handle the aging question and what adjustments have you made when life gets hard as you age? Signed, Peter."

"Peter: When I hear an older person sigh and say, 'life is hard,' I am always tempted to ask, 'compared to what?' But I don't. I know it's difficult for some people. For me personally, I have found that the older I get, the uglier I'm willing to go out in public. Hopefully, we'll all get older, we can't help that. But, Peter, we don't have to BE old."

"Noah: When is the full moon this month? Please forgive me for not knowing. Signed, Kathleen."

"Kathleen: I forgive you. However, you should forgive yourself for not knowing what you didn't know before you learned it."

"Noah: There is this old lady living next to us and she has this big tree with limbs hanging over the fence in my yard. All year long I'm having to rake up HER leaves and HER twigs from that tree that fall in my yard. I've warned her about it over the years but she won't do anything to fix it. Do I have the right to dump all the leaves and twigs back over the fence on to her property? That's only fair, isn't it? Signed, Lenny."

"Lenny: Listen, I'm a nice person so if I'm a butthole to you, you need to ask yourself why. LEAVE THAT OLD LADY ALONE!"

"Noah: I just heard that diamonds are not made from coal. Is that true? All my life I've heard that diamonds come from coal that has been pressurized over millions of years. Now they're telling us that isn't true? What else are they hiding from us? Signed, Henry."

"Henry: Everything! In moments of doubt, like these, trust your gut, hug your dog, and eat a donut."

"Noah: Just to be honest, I have to admit I hate people from a certain political party—I mean I hate them! They're stupid and ignorant and self-righteous morons. You can probably guess which party I'm referring to. I don't want to hate these people, but I can't seem to help myself. What can I do? Signed, Flabbergasted."

"Dear Sir: Unfortunately, you will not be able to change how people are—especially political people. However, there's always room for you to be a better person. Always."

EIGHTEEN

Noah finally made it home after the hike and a short visit to the Moab Brewery. He was very excited at the anticipation of an email from Ana—maybe two or three. He sat down in front of the screen and waited . . . finally, his account came up. Nothing but junk and more junk. He was heartbroken. He didn't know what to think. Ana had always written to him—every day she'd written to him. He thought about the hike and the four women and the ranger—she was nice. But he needed Ana.

Instead, he wrote a long, missive to the elusive Ana describing how much he missed her daily email. Then he deleted it before sending it. He didn't want to seem too needy, even though he was too needy.

℧℧℧

Ana stopped by the Slickrock Café on her way home but decided to only get a bagel and a cup of coffee. She, too, sat in front of her computer and wondered what she should say to Noah in her daily email. She couldn't be honest. She couldn't even tell a good lie. For the first time in her experience with Noah, she was completely without thought. She sat there, she took a long shower, she ate some ice cream—ice cream always made her feel better—but she still didn't know what to say.

She watched a Lifetime movie that didn't end until midnight. Then she looked at her computer and decided to write Noah a message that he would see in the morning:

"My dear Noah, I hope you're well. I almost forgot to write to you today; I was very busy at work. Some unforeseen circumstances arose that demanded my full attention. I hope you've had a good day and haven't forgotten about me. Please let me know how you are and write back as soon as you can.

Always, your Ana."

Two minutes after sending her message, before she could close her computer for the night, a message appeared from Noah:

"Ana, my lovely, I thought you'd forgotten about me. I was beginning to think one of those North Carolina hillbillies had swept you off your feet. I also had a busy day. I went on a hike in the desert to a place I hadn't been before. I want to say it was wonderful, but I kept daydreaming of one day meeting you and unfortunately I can't remember much of what I saw. Do you think the day will ever come when we will meet?"

"Of course, it will come, Noah. We must practice patience. Now tell me about your hike today. Did you go alone or with a friend?" Ana was trying to get some information from Noah; maybe he would say something about the "ranger" in his description of the day's hike.

"As I said, I've forgotten most of it because all I had on my mind was you, my lovely. I was dreaming of your blonde hair, or brown, or black, or whatever color it is this month. And of your face and legs and arms . . . you do have a face and legs and arms don't you, my dear? As for the hike itself, I went with a group of other hikers but I didn't know any of them."

"Yes, dear Noah, I have a face and arms and legs. And my hair color just changed slightly. I hope you'll like it. Did you and these other hikers go by yourselves on this dangerous trip into the unknown? Did one of you know the way so you wouldn't get lost?"

"Your hair color changed? Oh . . . my imagination is running wild at the possibilities. Our little group had a ranger from the park to lead us into the depths of the maze and the wild unknown. But if you come here, my dear, we won't need a ranger to guide us—I'll make sure you find your way and will promise to take good care of you and make it a memorable trip you won't soon forget."

Ana thought of other questions to ask. She needed to find out more what Noah thought about the "ranger," of course, the ranger being her. "Was this ranger a professional guide? Someone you could trust? I wouldn't want to place your welfare in the hands of an amateur. Describe the ranger to me so it'll ease my mind, dear Noah."

Noah thought this was an odd request. Why would she care about some unknown park ranger? But to make her happy, "Yes, our ranger was a thorough professional, dear Ana, no need for you to worry. In fact, our ranger was a lady ranger, who only got us lost a couple of times—lucky for our little group that I was there to lead us back to safety. She seemed to be a frightened little thing who gladly accepted my help."

Ana didn't like reading this part; however, she knew it just a man being a man—they always wanted to impress the girls. She also knew she couldn't push this any further without arousing too much suspicion, so she let it go. "Well, I'm glad you could save the group, dear Noah. You are such a brave soul. I'm going to bed now and I promise I won't wait till midnight tomorrow to write to you. Sweet dreams.

Always, your Ana."

Noah read the last email seven times. "Sweet dreams." "Always, your Ana." He read those parts eleven times. He started to write her back about the "going to bed" part but decided not to push it too far. He thought about it though. He thought about it a lot!

Ana had the next day off and decided to go to Main Street again and visit the Slickrock Café. It was nice getting out and sampling the various blends of coffee they had, plus the bagels and scones were delicious. Moab was a sleepy little town in the mornings before the tourists all woke up and flooded the streets in the afternoons.

Noah didn't sleep well at all. The email from Ana mentioning "going to bed" kept his mind spinning all night. He finally got up early, showered, got dressed, and went downtown himself. He needed to get out and get his mind off Ana. He had nowhere special in mind as he parked and walked down the street, but he'd always wanted to try the new coffee shop next to the book store. He walked in and smelled the coffee aromas which were heavenly to him. He ordered a large Especial and took a seat by the window to watch the traffic pass lazily by.

Ana parked her jeep on Main Street and started walking toward the Slickrock Café. She had to pass the new coffee shop on the way, and when she did she heard a knocking on the window. She stopped and looked in and saw Noah waving at her and holding up his coffee cup. Noah had seen her walking down the street and decided he'd invite her for coffee to show his appreciation for the nice hike yesterday. Ana froze. What to do? She had no choice, she had to go in.

Noah pulled out a seat for her as the waitress came over. Noah recommended the Especial, which she ordered, plus a scone for her and Noah. She waited for him to speak first,

"I really enjoyed the hike yesterday. You did a great job out there . . . thanks."

Ana had to remind herself that Noah didn't know who she was. Just stay calm and don't say anything stupid. "Glad you enjoyed it. I'm sorry, but I seem to have forgotten your name."

"It's Noah, but I never got your name yesterday. We all called you Ranger all day."

Ana's mind was spinning, she couldn't think. Finally, Noah continued, "That's okay, Ranger is fine with me. I probably wouldn't want to be telling weird looking strangers my name either."

Ana smiled just as the waitress brought her coffee. There was a moment or two of awkward silence as Ana poured milk into her cup, then she asked, "Do you live around here?"

"Yeah, out past the Brewery. You?"

Ana answered, "Yes, I've been living here about four years now. I came here from Zion National Park. I like Moab a lot better."

Noah thought to himself, "She's not really beautiful or anything, but she's got a nice smile and voice." He asked, "Are you married? You got a family here?"

Ana had to take a sip of coffee before answering. "No, never been married. You?"

Noah took a bite of his scone and said, "Nope. I guess we're sort of weird, aren't we? I mean most people have families or married or something."

Ana just nodded, without answering. Then she asked, "What sort of work do you do?"

"I work for the paper." He didn't really want to tell her it was the Salt Lake City Tribune. He'd rather people thought he worked for the local Moab Gazette.

Ana nodded again, wondering what else to say. They both ate their scones and sipped coffee while stealing looks at each other. She thought, "There is no way in the world this man would ever find me attractive."

Noah thought, "I bet she'd look okay if she put on some makeup." Then he asked, "Do you lead those hikes every week?"

She didn't lead the hikes every week. In fact, she only led this one because the other ranger was sick, but she told Noah, "Yeah, every week. Have a nice one coming up. You should join us again if you have the time." Then she immediately thought to herself, "Stupid girl! He probably thinks I'm asking him out on a hiking date."

Noah nodded and thought, "Did she just ask me out on a hiking date?" So he answered, "Yeah, I might do that."

Ana was so flummoxed with that answer that she suddenly rose, grabbing her scone and coffee, and replied, "Well, great, maybe I'll see you then. Thanks for the coffee, but I'm sorta late, I need to get going." Without waiting for a reply, she walked out the door and started walking the wrong way. When she realized it, she had to turn around and pass by the window where Noah was. He smiled and waved to her and thought, "Hmm, she has a nice walk."

NINETEEN

"Noah: I have some friends who go mountain climbing nearly every weekend but that scares me to death, so I don't go with them. Some other friends I have like to go sky-diving. My parents have a four-wheeler they take out in the desert. These things just scare me, so I don't go. Is something wrong with me? Signed, Billie."

"Billie: I totally understand your apprehensions; however, I personally think that fear is God's way of saying, 'Pay attention, this could be fun.'"

"Noah: Every morning I have a problem with my wife deciding who is going to do what about the kids. Then, I get to work and my boss always has an attitude and complains about everything I do. Finally, when I get home after work, my kids never do what I ask them to do and they're always creating problems and issues. Do you have any advice that might help me? Signed, Caden."

"My dear Caden: If everywhere you go there's a problem, guess what?"

"Noah: I'm a young, single adult who is working and supporting myself, but my parents keep trying to make all the decisions for me about my future. Even my grandfather is getting involved suggesting things I should do and not do. I'm about to scream! I'm so unhappy! I mean, it's my life and I think I should decide what I'm going to do—am I right? Signed, Casey."

"Casey: That's a tough one. I've always thought that old people will believe everything; middle-aged people, like your parents, suspect everything; and young people know everything. But, in your case, being happy is a very personal thing and it really has nothing to do with anyone else."

"Noah: You're always giving advice and criticizing everything we do. Why do you think you're going in the right direction and we're not? What do you look for in people that makes your life so much better than ours? Signed, Donald."

"Donald: I'm quite sure my life is not better than yours, or anyone's for that matter. But, to answer your question, I like people with a strong mind, an interesting mind, a twisted mind, and also people who can make me smile. Donald, I've found that it's not who you are that holds you back, it's who you think you're not."

"Noah: I'm changing my political party to 'none of the above.' I have never seen such an idiotic group of people in my life as the ones we have now running for office. I can't stand any of them. I think they'll say or do anything if it will help them get elected. Sorry to be so negative, but these people just yank my chain. What do you think about them? Signed, Ralph."

"Ralph: I think politicians are people who will find a perfectly clear, shallow stream, then muddy it all up just to make the water seem deep."

"Noah: My two best friends are very nice and we go back a long way, but they're so negative it's hard for me to be around them very long. They don't like their jobs, they're unhappy in their marriages, they hate all politicians—they don't like anything. I don't want to be like them but recently I've started being unhappy with things. I don't want to end up like them and hate everything. What should I do? Signed, Rachel."

"Rachel: If you're not happy you're doing something wrong. I know they're your friends, but my advice is to stay away from negative people. They have a problem for every solution."

"Noah: I need your help. My son and his wife travel all the time. I know they can't afford it; they don't make that much money. I'm worried they're being very irresponsible and if they decide to have kids, they won't have any savings to raise them properly. Don't you think they should be living within their means and be responsible in their lives? Signed, a concerned Mom."

"Mom: I'm not the right person to ask. I personally think anyone who lives within their means suffers from a lack of imagination. I can always make more money, but I cannot make more time."

"Noah: I'm an avid reader of action novels and thrillers. I love the authors Michael Connelly, Greg Iles, Lee Child, John Sandford, Lisa Scottoline, and CJ Box. I'm looking for another author I might like. Do you have a suggestion? If so, why do you like that author? Signed, Ida."

"My dear Ida: My personal favorite action-type author is Donald Charles. Why? Because last year he went on vacation to the Virgin Islands . . . and this year they are just the 'Islands.' He's that good."

TWENTY

Ana wondered if she should email Noah or not. She kept having to remind herself that he didn't know her as Ranger, only as Ana.

"My dear Noah, I hope you are well. What are you doing to keep yourself busy when you're not working? Are you planning any more hikes out into the wilderness?"

"Ana, my lovely, I'm busy preparing an itinerary for when you visit. As I told you before, we'll take a raft trip down the Colorado River, then we'll go on a long hike into the backcountry. Just you and me. But don't you be afraid, I'll protect you from the elements and from all the wild and dangerous beasts in the desert."

"Are you referring to the raft trip where you suggested I shouldn't bring my bathing suit with me?"

"I'm only looking out for your welfare, my lovely. If your bathing suit got wet and didn't dry properly, you could catch a cold. I'm only looking out for you, dear Ana."

"You are indeed a true gentleman, Noah. So, I'm guessing if I don't wear a bathing suit, then neither would you. Is that correct? It would be very noble of you not to wear your suit in the frigid waters of the river. I've heard that cold water can be very revealing at times."

Noah read that last email and wondered if Ana was messing with him or being serious. He decided to skirt the issue and move on to another subject. "Ana, I was wondering if I came to North Carolina on my vacation, if you would have enough time to see me for a day or two. What do you think?"

"Noah, you know I'd always try my best to work you into my schedule, however hectic it might be. Usually, I can find twenty or thirty minutes on my lunch break. Unfortunately, we don't have any wild, roaring rivers here, or dangerous, life-threatening hikes to go on. I'm afraid North Carolina would bore you to tears. It would probably work out best if I could somehow travel to Utah and visit you at some time in the future. What do you think?"

"I think that would be awesome! When can you come? I'll start arranging everything and working out the details. Do you like coffee or tea in the mornings, my dear?"

"You aren't inferring that we'll be staying together on this vacation are you, my dear, sweet, innocent Noah?"

"Of course not, my lovely. I'm only asking so that I can have the correct breakfast drink delivered to your door. I would never imply anything else. I thought you knew me better than that."

"Please excuse me, Noah, for reading between the lines and wishing for something that I know you would never be capable of. It's your true gentleman's nature that keeps me interested. It's just that . . . well, you know, sometimes a girl dreams."

Noah knew alright. He could barely sit still as he thought of the dreams and possibilities.

The week drug by as Noah and Ana played with each other via email. Each going to the edge and backing away. Each pushing the limits of their imaginations and seeing how much they could get away with. Each wishing the other would step over the edge.

Friday night, after the last email, Noah decided he would go again out to Canyonlands and take the guided hike with the lady ranger he'd met before. She was nice to talk with and maybe a long hike would help distract his mind and thoughts from Ana for a few hours. He drove out Saturday morning and found only two other vehicles in the parking lot. One was a National Park SUV and the other was an old battered Jeep. He parked and gathered his backpack, making sure he had water and some snacks, then went into the park office.

He saw an older, gray-headed man milling about, but didn't see the ranger anywhere. Noah was hoping this old guy wasn't the person leading the hike today. Just then Ana came from the back office. She looked different today. Her hair was styled and she had on makeup. She also had on fairly short shorts, to be a ranger's uniform. Noah didn't mind. He had thought she might have nice legs and he was happy to see he was correct.

The old guy's name was Herbert. He had a large backpack, a hiking stick, expensive hiking boots, and a large, wide-brimmed hat. He looked like a professional hiker. Ana also told Herbert to simply call her Ranger, as they started on their journey. She led the way, with Herbert following and Noah in the rear. After about an hour and a half, Herbert suddenly stopped and said, "Well, that's it for me. I'll be going back now. Thanks for the hike, Ranger. You two have fun."

Noah couldn't believe what was happening. Herbert simply turned around and started back down the trail. He wasn't sure if the hike was over or what was going on. Ana looked at him and asked, "Do you want to continue?"

Noah said, "Yeah, unless you'd rather not."

"No, it's a beautiful day and there's a small waterfall near the end I'd like to see . . . if you're interested."

Noah took a drink of water and replied, "Let's go."

As they started down the trail Noah had a great opportunity to notice Ana's legs and her walk and her behind. He liked what he was seeing. He was thinking to himself, "I don't remember her looking this good before. But, she's really not that pretty. Nice legs but that's all." Just then, Ana turned around and smiled at Noah, saying, "I think you're really going to like this hike today. Let me know if you need to stop for water or anything."

Noah said, "I'm good for now, but I'll let you know." And again thought to himself, "Is it the makeup that's making her smile look so good? There's something different about her today."

There was something different. Ana had lightened her hair just a bit, she had carefully applied some makeup to give her that "glow" that Revlon promised on the box, and she painted her fingernails. She also took her park ranger shorts to a seamstress and had them shortened, tightened, and altered. She knew her legs and bottom were probably her best assets and she wanted Noah to notice them. He did.

Neither of them spoke much on the hike. When they took their first water break, Ana was still a little too intimidated to initiate any conversation. Noah was busy eating some Reece's Pieces and almonds, while he tried to look at Ana's legs, without letting her know he was looking at her legs. She knew.

When they arrived at the small waterfall at the end of the trail, they both took off their backpacks and leaned against some rocks while they rested. Noah peeled and ate an orange. Ana only drank from a thermos. Noah didn't know what was in the flask and didn't ask. Normally, he would have dug a small hole in the dirt and buried his orange peels, but because of Ana's presence, he put them back in his pack. They stared at the little waterfall until Noah finally said, "This is great out here. Glad I came."

Ana wanted to say, "I'm glad you came, too." But instead, she answered, "Yeah, it's nice out here. Not too many people know about this area."

She tried to sneak glances of Noah as he ate his orange. She liked the way his Adam's apple went up and down as he swallowed. Noah tried to look at her upper thighs, where the shorts stopped, but it was hard without her noticing. After a few moments of silence, Ana said, "Well, I guess we'd better be on our way." Quickly, Noah hopped up and extended his hand towards Ana to help her up. She hesitated, then grabbed his hand as he pulled her up. When she was standing, they both took an extra second to actually let go of each other's hand. It was a bit awkward, but it was also a bit exciting.

After that, they hiked in silence nearly all the way back to the parking lot. As they came around the last bend in the trail, Ana said, "Well, here we are. Hope you enjoyed it."

Noah looked into her eyes and thought, "Dang, she's a lot prettier than I thought she was." He was still looking at her when she added,

"Did you like it?"

"Like what?"

"The hike. Did you like the hike?"

"Oh," Noah said. Somehow he had become confused. "Yeah, it was great. Thanks."

Ana smiled, then nodded and turned to walk into the ranger station. She didn't want to leave Noah, but she didn't know what else to say or do. Noah didn't want her to leave either but was afraid of what he'd say or do. So she went inside and peeked out the blinds again. Noah went to his car thinking, "What just happened?"

TWENTY-ONE

"Noah: I'm sick and tired of watching all these pampered, rich professional athletes every night on television. How can it be right for them to be making twenty or thirty million dollars a year for playing a sport? Look at all the homeless and disadvantaged out there and then you see these prima donnas dancing around on television laughing and playing. It disgusts me seeing this every night. Signed, Adam."

"Adam: Quit watching."

"Noah: I went to Canada on vacation last month and was shopping in a bookstore where I leafed through a geography book of Canada. Did you know that in Canada they have maps that show the United States on top and Canada at the bottom? I think they're actually teaching their kids this. Can you believe it? Signed, Sammy."

"Sammy: As long as you both enjoy it, does it really matter who's on top and who's on bottom?

"Noah: I have a brother who is worthless. He ignores us all and never visits. He treats my dad like dirt and the rest of us even worse. My dad still has him in his will, however, and we all hate this. Is there any way we can get my brother eliminated from my dad's will? He doesn't deserve a penny for the way he has treated us all. There must be something we can do. Signed, Chrissy."

"Chrissy: Be grateful. Eat more vegetables. Love more . . . worry less."

"Noah: I am now firmly convinced that you are a jackass! I bet you won't print this in your silly column. Signed, Frank."

"Frank: Here you go, it's printed. And you taught me a valuable lesson: Some humans are really bad at being human."

"Noah: Why do these stupid school buses have to stop every hundred yards? Can't these lazy kids walk a hundred yards? It's ridiculous! These stupid buses are making me extremely unhappy. Help! Signed, Victoria."

"Victoria: Calm down and don't do anything crazy. I know today's kids didn't have to walk six miles, uphill, to school each day like we did. Life just isn't fair. One secret to happiness, Victoria, is not to do what you like to do, but to learn to like what you have to do."

"Noah: Nearly every week you write something about drinking. Do you have a problem with alcohol? Signed, Ginny."

"Ginny: You're very observant. I used to have a drinking problem, but now I make enough money."

"Noah: You beat around the bush a lot. What do you really think about our country and all the people living here? Be honest. Signed, Kelly."

"Kelly: Okay, here's what I think: We live in a generation of emotionally weak people. Everything has to be watered down because it's offensive, including the truth."

"Noah: I just made a delivery yesterday at an office downtown and there were several hundred people protesting something in front of a government building. Don't these people work? How do they live? I see this nearly every week. Signed, Isaac."

"Isaac: The problem we face today is that the people who work for a living are outnumbered by those who vote for a living."

"Noah: Tell us something profound and wise today—your keys to happiness! Signed, Lorna."

"Lorna: I have discovered that most of us get old too soon and smart too late. And my personal key to happiness is very simple: Stay away from buttholes."

TWENTY-TWO

Ana was now in a major quandary. She had the unknowing Noah emailing her every day as he thought of her as Ana. Then, she also had the known Noah taking hikes with her each week as he thought of her as Ranger. She felt very strongly that the unknowing Noah, who thought of her as Ana, was falling in love with her via email. She knew she was falling in love with him—email or no email.

She also had a strong suspicion that the short time Noah and she grasped hands on the trail that something happened. It certainly did for her and she was hoping it did for him as well. After that, he looked at her differently, and not just at her legs either. Her two biggest issues now were first, how to see him in person more than once a week, and second, what to do about her name—he couldn't keep calling her Ranger.

The following day she sat in her office and finished up some paperwork. Mostly she daydreamed, but she kept the door closed so no one else could tell. The unknowing Noah and the knowing Noah dominated her consciousness. She was called out to the entrance station once to help a tourist who had run out of gas. The closest gas station was back in Moab about an hour away. She let the tourist buy five gallons from the park's underground supply, but with a stern warning to him to be aware of his own vehicle. This desolate, remote area was not the sort of place to run out of gas or supplies.

After work, she drove back to Moab but was not interested in going home. She was hoping if she walked down Main Street maybe Noah would see her again—a girl could dream. She walked up one side then down the other, but no Noah. She finally settled in at the Slickrock Café for a salad and a cup of coffee—with key lime pie for dessert. She sat near the window and searched the streets for

Noah's car to no avail. She finally gave up and sulked back home where she was certain she'd have an email or two from him.

She only had one, but it was a good one:

"My dearest, elusive Ana, I have a vacation coming up soon and I am determined to meet you once and for all. If I have to come to North Carolina and visit every town in that state, I am steadfast and resolved in my pursuit of locating you. Or, you can come visit my beautiful state and I will treat you like royalty. Not only will I take you on breath-taking hikes into the wilderness, and adventurous river journeys, I will also entertain you to the point where you'll probably never want to leave.

"I have decided, dear Ana, that we must meet to finally confirm what we both already know—we are meant for other. That is, of course, that you're not expecting Brad Pitt or Bradley Cooper. No, my dear, I am but an average columnist, with an above average desire to finally meet the girl of my dreams. So, what will it be, my dear? Must I come there and roam the cities and towns for you? Or, will you come and visit me, with the possibility of you never wanting to leave once you experience paradise? Waiting faithfully and eternally for your answer, Noah."

"Oh, no . . . what do I do now?" This was all Ana could think of as she read the email over and over. What do I tell Noah about this? How can I put him off for a while? Then, she started thinking, if I can be sure he likes ME and not some imaginary pen pal, I'll just break it off with him online. I need more time! I need to be sure he likes me, Ranger, and not me, the phantom Ana.

☾☾☾

Noah went to his favorite hangout, the Moab Brewery, to reflect on the email he just sent to Ana. Before his Back-of-Beyond Burger arrived, someone slapped him on the back and shook the table so badly it almost spilled his Black Raven Stout. Noah looked up and saw his old friend Duncan smiling broadly at him. Duncan worked for a mining outfit and had been out on a project for the last three months. He was really the only close friend Noah had in Moab. Noah and Duncan, who was also single, had closed down the bars many nights in the past. Duncan loved the women but was never able to get serious with one. He'd been engaged once in the past, but he got cold feet and ended it.

"Duncan, when did you get back in town? Why didn't you call?"

"No need to call, I knew I'd find you in here. You're pretty predictable, my old friend."

"How long will you be around before they ship you out again?

Duncan thought a moment, then said, "I think I'll be here for a good while now, or until they locate a new source of revenue outside the state."

They told stories and lies and re-lived past experiences while sipping their stouts and eating burgers. The conversation finally got around to women. Duncan asked who was keeping his friend busy lately. Noah answered, "Duncan, I can hardly explain this, but I've met this woman online that I think I might be in love with. She's smart and witty and we just seem to complement each other. I can't wait to get home every day and read her emails—she's all I think about."

Duncan was nodding and smiling as his friend described his feelings, then he asked, "What's her name?"

Noah swallowed before answering, then said, "It might be Ana . . . but I'm not sure."

"You're not sure what her name is?"

"It's complicated."

"It's so complicated that you don't know her name? Really?"

"Well . . . "

Before he could continue, Duncan asked, "How old is she?"

"I'm not really certain about her age."

Duncan looked at his friend like he was speaking Chinese with a Russian accent. "What does she look like?"

"Umm, that one is a little hard to answer."

"What do you mean, hard to answer? Just tell me what she looks like."

Noah scrunched up his face a little, thought about lying to his friend, then finally said, "I haven't actually met her yet."

Duncan nodded, then asked, "But you've seen her picture, right?"

"Well . . . not exactly."

Duncan took a long pull from his beer, leaned his head slightly to the left, then asked, "You don't know what she looks like, but you think you might be in love with her? Is that right?"

"Yeah, I guess."

"Where does this young lady live?"

Noah then took a long pull from his beer and started sweating a little as he answered, "I'm not really sure, maybe North Carolina."

Duncan sat there staring at his friend in disbelief. "So, you're telling me that you think you're in love with a young lady that you've never seen, and you don't know her name or how old she is, and she may live in North Carolina but you're not sure. Is that about right?"

Noah did not want to answer that question. Noah knew his answer was not what Duncan wanted to hear. In fact, Noah knew his answer made no sense at all . . . but he couldn't help it. "Yes."

TWENTY-THREE

Noah sat at his desk ready to start the morning column and answering questions his readers had sent in. He was still questioning himself and wondering what his friend Duncan was thinking about him. All he was sure of was that "yes"; he did feel that way about Ana. So what if he didn't know what she looked like, or how old she was, or what her true name was, or even where she lived . . . so what? That's what he sat there thinking . . . so what?

"Noah: My doctor tells me I need to start exercising more. I joined a gym about a year ago and met several people and have been taking notice of quite a few more people over the last year. From what I see, going to a gym hasn't changed any of these people. The fat ones are still fat, the skinny ones aren't any stronger, and the ugly ones are still ugly. So, my question is: What's the point of going to a gym? Signed, Harold."

"Harold: I'm probably not the right person to answer that question; however, if your doctor suggested going to the gym, then I would defer to his better judgment. But after reading your message to me, the more you explain it, the more I don't understand it."

"Noah: I have this snooty friend who speaks a little French, which she always tries to work in conversations just to let everyone know that she can. Sometimes I'd like to take her French and stuff it where the sun doesn't shine, if you know what I mean. Signed, Betty."

"Dear sweet Betty: I've always found that the ability to speak in several languages is an asset, but the ability to keep your mouth shut in any language is priceless."

"Noah: My grandmother used to tell us all these old sayings which were so helpful. I'm trying to accumulate these sayings into a book. Do you have any things you were told that might be helpful? Signed, Loretta."

"Loretta: Yes, I remember one thing my dad always reminded me of. He said, 'Son, if your palm itches, you're going to get something. If your crotch itches, you've already got it."

"Noah: I have this girlfriend who loves to try and put me down whenever she can. I don't know why I'm still friends with her, but I am. She's always making fun of me and belittling me. Why does she do this? I mean, I'm her friend! Signed, very disappointed."

"Very Disappointed: Read this very carefully: No one can make you feel inferior without your consent."

"Noah: I want to know what you think. I wear a size 12 dress (I used to wear 8's or 10's.) I think I look great but my husband thinks I need to lose some weight. My mom also thinks I look great as do all my friends who, by the way, are bigger than me. My question is, knowing my dress size, do you think I'm fat? Signed, Laura."

"Laura: There is no way in the world I'm going to answer that question. First, I've never seen you. Second, I'm not going to give half my readers a reason to get mad at me. And, third, Laura, you don't have to be perfect to be amazing. However, I will add this ladies--if you THINK you're fat, you probably are."

"Noah: A women's group that I'm a member of keeps planning all these protests around town. Some are fine but some are rather crazy in my opinion. I like these girls and want to stay involved but I find a lot of the stuff they do doesn't make any sense. I'm feeling like it's more about politics and either CNN or Fox news than either right or wrong any longer. I hate to quit the group but it's just hard for me to participate much longer. Signed, Patsy."

"Patsy: Turn off the news and love your neighbor. You can always be a good person with a kind heart and still say no. One more thing, Patsy. Anything that costs you your peace of mind is too expensive."

"Noah: I screwed up the financials this week and my boss got really pissed. Then I turned in my report late and held up the accountants. I hope what I've always heard is correct: 'two wrongs make a right.' What do you think?" Signed, Tommy."

"Tommy: Two wrongs do not make it right, but two margaritas usually do."

"Noah: Why?" Signed, Albert."

"Albert: Why? Because the truth will set you free, but first it will piss you off. That's why."

TWENTY-FOUR

Noah and his friend Duncan met each night of the week at the Brewery as they renewed their friendship. Noah asked Duncan to come with him on the hike he was planning this weekend with the ranger lady. At first, Duncan didn't really want to go—he was more of an off-roader than a hiker. But when Noah described the ranger who led the hikes, describing her legs and bottom and her nice smile, Duncan changed his mind.

In preparation of the weekend hike Ana had her hair done to add some body to it and make it a little wavy, instead of the straight, dark locks of her native Robeson County heritage. With her new shortened ranger shorts, her new hairstyle, her new makeup package, and her naturally tanned-looking skin tones, she was very confident she could entice Noah into more than hiking with her. She was at the park headquarters at least an hour early and was hoping no one else but Noah would show up. Today's hike was to wind its way down to the Escalante River and follow its course through the canyon.

When Noah and Duncan arrived at the ranger station there were four other cars there in addition to the ranger's vehicle. Inside the headquarters, they found the same older man from last week, who only hiked an hour and a half, then turned around. There was also a younger couple and two college-aged guys who were all waiting on Ana to begin the hike. Ana had no intention of starting the hike until Noah showed up. All the introductions were made and the little group started off, Ana leading the way, the older guy next, then the two college guys, followed by the young married couple, then Duncan and Noah in the rear.

After the first quarter mile, Duncan told Noah he was going up to hike behind the ranger—he wanted a better look at her legs. The older guy didn't really like Duncan moving in front of him; he also liked the way Ana walked but he didn't want to say anything. The young couple was still in love and oblivious to everything as they held hands nearly the entire way, while the two college guys were busy looking at rocks and cactus along the trail. It was unclear what their purpose was. Noah followed them all while trying to catch glimpses of Ana's legs as well. He thought she had done something to her hair, but he wasn't sure.

At the first break, the older guy again turned around and went back to his car. As they all sat down and had a snack and some water, Duncan sat next to Ana and started asking questions as fast as he could: "How long does it take us to get to the river? How much elevation change is there? How deep do you think the river will be today?" He was trying his best to ingratiate himself with Ana. Her walk, her smile, and her general appearance had totally overwhelmed Duncan. Ana answered his questions, but her main objective was to sit and arrange her legs so that Noah could see her best assets. Duncan was simply a hindrance in her main goal today.

When they started the hike again, there was a gradual increase in elevation which winded Duncan so much that he couldn't ask Ana any more questions. She took advantage of this and scampered up several yards ahead of the group. They eventually got to the river, or more accurately a stream, and stopped under a cottonwood tree to have lunch and rest. Duncan was so tired that he couldn't ask a lot of questions to Ana; he just stared at her. He was smitten.

Noah noticed his enchantment and asked him, "You like her, huh?"

"She's gorgeous! I'd let her hike in my canyon any day."

Noah didn't see gorgeous, but he did see something in the ranger that he hadn't seen before. She had the kind of beauty that wasn't obvious when you first met her. It was something that you became aware of the more you were around her. He couldn't describe it, but he certainly could see it. Duncan was totally taken with her. He asked Noah, "Do you know if she's involved with anyone?"

"I have no idea. I only know that she's not married . . . she told me that."

"I'm gonna ask her out."

"Well don't do it out here! What if she says no? At least wait till we get back to the car."

Duncan nodded, but he wasn't sure if he could wait. Noah could tell he was still thinking about it, so he added, "Duncan, buddy, don't do anything out here. Wait till we get back, then you can do whatever you want. Okay?" In deference to his friend, Duncan agreed. But as soon as they arrived at the headquarters, he was going to ask her out.

The rest of the hike was fine. The young couple left the trail a few times to be alone—nobody cared. The two college guys picked up a few rocks but Ana had to warn them not to pick up any arrowheads or artifacts if they saw them. It was against park regulations. Duncan stayed as close to Ana as he could and Noah again brought up the rear.

When they arrived back at the park headquarters, Ana pulled her cell phone out as they walked the final few yards and was talking on it. When the group came up to her she said, "I've just had a call and I have to meet the medical team over at the White Rim trail for an emergency. Thanks for coming out today and I hope you enjoyed it. I need to run. Bye."

She hopped in her SUV and took off, leaving Duncan frustrated at the lost opportunity. Ana knew something was up with him and she didn't want to hang around and see what. He was a little too chummy and much too attentive on the way back. She sensed something and didn't want to chance that might happen. Thus, the imaginary phone call from the imaginary emergency. As she drove away she was thinking what a lost opportunity this day had been. Her hair looked great, her makeup held together all day, and her shorts were perfect, but she was never able to speak with Noah because of this crazy friend of his. What a lost day!

☾☾☾

Duncan was very frustrated. He liked the ranger girl. He liked her a lot. Her walk, her legs, her smile, he liked it all, and he was certain she liked him as well. He bugged Noah all the way back to Moab about her. "Why do you call her ranger? What's her real name?"

"That's what she goes by. She's never told us her real name."

"What's going on with you and women who won't tell you their real name, Noah? That's very weird. First, this girl you're so in love with, now the ranger."

"First of all, I never asked the ranger what her name was . . . okay? She just told us to call her ranger. Second, I'm not sure that Ana's name isn't Ana. I just don't know for sure."

Duncan nodded and added, "Well, I don't care what her name is, I'm gonna ask her out. Did you see those legs?"

"Don't you think you should try to find out something about her first? Like, does she have a boyfriend? Or, a girlfriend? Check that out before you go making a fool of yourself in front of her."

Duncan nodded again and said, "Good idea. You can do that for me, buddy. You talk to her and find out everything I need to know. Great idea!"

Noah said, "What? I'm not doing that. I barely know her. Besides these hikes I've only shared a cup of coffee with her one time in my life."

"Good. Do the coffee thing again and find out if she has a boyfriend. Good idea, Noah."

"No, it's not a good idea. Why do I let you talk me into this stuff? You're buying the beer tonight."

"For those legs, buddy, I'll buy the beer every night."

Ana was so distraught over the entire day that when she got home her intention was to email Noah and tell him the entire, crazy truth. Admit to everything, tell him who she was, and see what happened. Why couldn't Noah show her the attention that his friend had? It only proved that she simply was not good enough for him. She wasn't what he was looking for. She started to cry and she couldn't stop. But she didn't write the email either. She couldn't . . . she just couldn't.

TWENTY-FIVE

It took Noah three days sitting in the small coffee shop on Main Street to finally see the ranger walking by the store. When he did recognize her she was almost past the window before he realized it was her. He jumped up, leaving his coffee on the table, and ran outside the door calling her name, "Ranger, Ranger . . . remember me, Noah?"

Ana nearly fainted when he called her. She hadn't emailed him in three days because she just didn't know what to say. Noah had probably written her twenty-five times during the last three days. He seemed heartbroken. But not today; he was smiling as he ran to catch up to her. Ana regained her composure and answered, "Yes, I do remember, how are you?"

"I was just having a cup of coffee in the shop back there. Do you have time to join me?"

Ana had all the time in the world for Noah, so she answered, "I guess so . . . is everything alright?"

"Yeah, sure. It would be nice to have a little company if you have time."

They walked back to the little shop and went in but Noah's coffee was gone. The girl cleaning tables was very efficient. Noah ordered two more cups as they sat by the window. Noah noticed the ranger's hair was a little different, but he couldn't tell exactly why. Also, she wasn't wearing any makeup, not even lipstick.

As Ana sat down she realized she hadn't applied any makeup this morning. She was only going down to the drug store and never dreamed she'd see anyone she knew—especially Noah. She was both nervous and excited as she added a little cream to her coffee. They stumbled a bit about the weather and the hike last weekend, then Noah jumped in with the real reason he'd stopped her. "Remember my friend from the hike last week, Duncan?"

Immediately, Ana thought to herself, "Oh, no." It was all she could do to keep smiling as she answered, "Yeah, I think so."

"Well, he really liked you and wondered if you were involved with anyone right now. He'd like to ask you out." Noah took a sip of his coffee and thought he noticed a small twitch in the ranger's face.

Ana was urging herself, "Think girl, think!" What does she say? If she says "no" then this goofy friend of Noah's is going to ask her on a date. If she says "yes" she is seeing someone, then they'll both probably never come on a hike again with her and she'll never see Noah again.

As she's trying to figure out how to answer that question, Noah asks, "Well, yes or no?"

Ana stumbled a little and finally answered, "Not right now. I was seeing someone but it didn't work out." She simply couldn't take the chance of Noah not coming on any more hikes with her. In her mind, there was always the chance things could change between them. She couldn't give up her dream, she just couldn't.

"So, you don't mind if he asks you out then? Is that right?"

Again, Ana stumbled a little, but said, "No, it's alright."

They both sipped their coffee while they figured out what to say next. Noah got a good look at her as she played with her coffee cup and he thought, "She might look better without makeup."

Ana was fiddling with her cup and thought, "Stupid girl, tell him you're his Ana. Quit being a fool."

But before she could finish those admonitions, Noah asked, "Do you mind telling me your name? All we know is Ranger unless your parents were really weird and named you that."

"Oh, my gosh. Oh, my gosh. Oh, my gosh." Ana hadn't thought of this; what does she do? Her head was spinning, but then she thought, "What difference does it make, he doesn't know me anyway."

"My name is Dorothy, which I'm not overly fond of. That's why I tell people to call me Ranger. I dislike Dot even more than Dorothy. In high school, some of the guys started calling me Wiz, after the movie Wizard of Oz. The guys at the park headquarters call me Tana because my skin seems so tanned all the time."

Noah smiled at her as she said this; he enjoyed the little personal story. When she finished, she smiled back at him and he realized that, yes, she does look better without makeup. A lot better. He hoped Ana would look this good when he finally meets her.

When they left the coffee shop, Noah wandered back to his car wondering why Ana had stopped emailing him. He'd go home before he started work and email her again—he couldn't give up on his dream. Ana wandered back to her car in a daze. She completely forgot about going to the drug store. She might have to go on a date with this Duncan guy, but at least she was pretty sure Noah would continue their weekly hikes together.

Noah stared at the computer screen and started typing. "My dear, sweet Ana . . . have I done something to hurt you? I can't figure out why you've stopped writing to me. Whatever the reason, please let me know and I'll fix it. You know how much I need you in my life now. How much I look forward to your messages every day. You must know how badly I want us to meet. I feel there is a bond between us that is really special. I know you feel the same way—don't you? Please write to me, dear, Ana. I miss you so much, always your Noah."

TWENTY-SIX

"Noah: You're a man, right? Why are men so stupid? Signed, Danelle."

"Danelle: How does a shepherd count his flock without falling asleep?

Why do all the days of the week end in 'Y'?

Do pigs pull hamstrings?

Has anyone actually killed two birds with one stone?

Why do old men have hair in their ears?

Why are things 'typed up' but 'written down'?

"Yes, Danelle, there are many unanswerable questions; however, there are only two things I've found that are infinite: the universe and the stupidity of men, and I'm not sure about the universe."

"Noah: I just drove my family to Kansas City to visit my mom and dad. I drove all the way across Kansas and it is the most boring place I've ever seen. Why would anybody want to live there? Signed, Matt."

"Matt: Chocolate doesn't ask silly questions like this . . . chocolate understands."

"Noah: If you were President and could change any ONE thing about our country, what would it be? Signed, Abraham."

"Abraham: I've thought quite a bit about your question and here's my answer: I would make our country more compassionate. Compassion is a language the deaf can hear and the blind can see, whereas war does not determine who is right, only who is left."

"Noah: Logically, do you think there are still witches alive today? If so, where are they? Signed, Sharon."

"Sharon: Logic will only take you from A to B. Your imagination will take you everywhere."

"Noah: Can you please let your readers know how important it is to close the lids on their trash cans. If not, crows can get in the trash can and mess it all up. Thanks for your help. Signed, Marvin."

"Marvin: I sure will. I do not want my trash to get messed up. As my dad always told me, 'one man with courage makes a majority.'"

"Noah: If you have x-ray vision, and can see through anything, wouldn't you see through everything and actually see nothing?" Signed, Oliver."

"Oliver: Drink like no one is watching. Or dance. Whatever."

"Noah: I'm getting older and have a bum knee. It's hard for me to walk most days. Tell me why drugstores make sick people walk all the way to the back of the store to get our prescriptions while healthy people can buy cigarettes at the front? Signed, Dwight."

"Dwight: I don't know about drugstores, but I do know something about getting older. First, you forget names, then you forget faces.

Next, you forget to pull your zipper up, and finally, you forget to pull it down."

"Noah: I have a friend who thinks she knows everything, but if I tell her that she's being judgmental, aren't I being judgmental myself?" Signed, Erica."

"Erica: So far, I've survived 100% of my worst days and some things are just not important."

"Noah: Since you're so smart, answer this: If it's zero degrees outside today and it's supposed to be twice as cold tomorrow, how cold is it going to be? Signed, Ivan."

"Ivan: If Jimmy cracks corn and no one cares, why does he keep doing it?"

"Noah: If a man is rich but has no friends or family to enjoy it with, or a man has many friends and family but is poor, what's the difference between them, or are they the same theoretically? Signed, Jonas."

"Jonas: Very interesting question. In my experience I've found that a rich man is nothing but a poor man with money."

"Noah: My boyfriend and I have been dating for fifteen months and he has never brought up marriage at any time in our relationship. I think it's time I should say something or at least drop some hints. After all, a man is not complete unless he's married . . . right? Signed, Lois."

"Lois: You might be right. A man is incomplete until he is married. After that, he's finished."

"Noah: My fourteen-year-old son is listening to this nasty music on the radio with curse words and worse. Then he plays these idiotic video games all night before he goes to bed. Every week he's getting harder and harder to handle. Our society is churning out an entire generation of disrespectful kids and I don't know what the solution is. What is happening to our society? Signed, a very, very concerned Mom."

"Concerned Mom . . . . Respect is taught at home! If your kid is a disrespectful little twerp, it's your fault. Not society's, not music, not video games! YOURS!

"Noah: We have a small group that gets together each week and plays chess with each other. You seem like a smart guy (sometimes). Would you like to join our chess group? Signed, Harvey."

"Harvey: I used to play chess with my friend Jerry all the time, and one day he said, 'Let's make this more interesting.' So we stopped playing chess."

TWENTY-SEVEN

Ana had to come up with some reason why she hadn't written Noah in three days, but nothing made sense. She finally wrote him saying her computer had died and she only now had gotten it repaired. Noah was gullible and in love, so he believed it. At least Ana hadn't given Noah her phone number, so she shouldn't be expecting any phone calls from Duncan. She was wrong. Once Noah had her name, it was easy for him and Duncan to get her phone number. Ana's phone rang and she answered, "Hello."

Duncan asked, "Is this Dorothy?"

"Yes, who is this?"

"It's Duncan . . . Noah's friend."

Ana was stunned. She didn't know how to respond. After a few silent moments, Duncan asked, "Are you still there?"

"Uh, yes, I was busy with something when the phone rang. How did you get my number?"

"That was easy. We just checked out the website of the national park and found your whole name and called information."

Ana dejectedly said, "Oh."

"If this isn't a good time, I can call back later."

Ana started to tell him he was bothering her, but she didn't. "No, it's okay. How can I help you?"

"Well, I know you're busy, so I'll just get to the point. Would you like to go to dinner with me Saturday night?"

All Ana could think was, "Crap, crap, crap, crap, crap!" But remembering Noah, she answered, "Sure, that would be fun. Call me later with the details. I really need to get going now, I'm running a little late." She wasn't running late, but she couldn't talk any longer.

Duncan hung up thinking to himself, "I knew it! I knew she liked me." He called Noah right away and told him the news. "Hey, buddy. I was right. She jumped all over it, just like she'll jump all over me Saturday night. I can't understand why you haven't nailed her already."

Noah thought to himself, "Ana . . . that's why." But he answered, "Good news, buddy. When are you going out?"

"Saturday night. I'm going to take her to that new steak place down near the brewery."

Noah thought a moment, then asked, "Saturday? Are you still going on the hike with me on Saturday?"

Duncan hadn't remembered that. "No, I probably won't go now. I wouldn't want to get her too excited and get everyone lost. Just make sure she doesn't get hurt. Okay?"

ᗯᗯᗯ

"Dearest Noah, my computer seems to be okay now. I hope you are as well. I've missed you! Tell me what you've been doing with your time, besides working."

"Ana, my lovely, all I do with my time is think of you. What you're doing, what you look like, what color your hair is. Where you live. When you're coming to visit me. You know—all the usual questions."

"Oh, Noah, you know you're always in my thoughts and dreams. Do you ever dream of me?"

"I dream of you all day and all night . . . you know that."

"You dream of me all night, Noah? What on earth would you be dreaming about all night long?"

"Oh, you know . . . what book you're reading. What you had for dinner. What your favorite color is. If you pull for UNC or Duke.

Those things are very important to me, Ana, that's what I dream about."

"Really?"

"No."

"Well then tell me, dear Noah, what DO you dream about when you dream of me?"

"Honestly?"

"I thought we were always honest with each other, Noah."

"Yes, Ana, we are . . . I think."

"Well then, tell what you dream about at night, when you dream of me."

"Okay, I'll tell you, Ana, but remember, you asked me to be honest. I dream about sitting in the Moab Brewery and someone asking me why I'm drinking so much. I answer, 'I drink because I'm lonely, and I'm lonely because I drink.' Then I wake up and you're gone."

No immediate answer from Ana. Noah sat there about twenty minutes until an email finally appeared from her. "So, when you dream of me, you dream of sitting in a bar?"

"Initially . . . yes."

"Then what?"

"Then I think about ravaging your body, slowly, fastly, intermediately, and lastingly (I know those might not be real words—but it is my dream). Then, Ana, I dream you start to . . . and I wake up."

"Oh, Noah, you're making me blush."

"Why are you blushing, my lovely?"

"Because you're having the same dream I've been having . . . except I don't wake up so quickly."

TWENTY-EIGHT

"Noah: Where do I go to get free stuff? Signed, Leonardo."

"Leonardo: Keep going dude, you're getting there."

"Noah: I'm having trouble meeting a nice girl. I have a good job, I'm not crazy, I'm not an alcoholic, I keep in shape, but I just can't seem to meet anyone. What can I do? Signed, Roger."

"Roger, my friend: Someone you haven't even met yet is wondering what it'd be like to know someone like you."

"Noah: I work in an office downtown and it's starting to wear on me. I like the company, I like the work, but the people I work with just don't seem to like me; they're very cliquish. Have you ever had a job like this? Signed, Aaron."

"Aaron: It's okay if people don't like you. Most people don't even like themselves."

"Noah: My best friend is a lazy slob. I can say that because he's my friend. He's always falling into money; anything he invests in skyrockets. Girls come on to him. He wears the same dirty jeans and sometimes the same dirty shirts. He never washes his car or combs his hair. It's totally unbelievable! Have you ever heard of anyone like him? Signed, Johnson."

"Johnson: Sounds like you might be a tad jealous. A lot of us know people like your friend. I knew a guy once who was so lazy that he married a pregnant woman."

"Noah: I'm a total believer in love. I believe all the sayings about love: 'love will set you free,' 'all you need is love,' 'what the world needs now is love.' We all need more love in us and in the world. Yet, I never hear you say you are in love, my friend. Are you? Signed, Lovely Linda."

"Lovely Linda: I'm very sorry to admit it, but if love were oil, I'd be about a quart low."

"Noah: I don't think you get it. Some of us aren't lucky enough to go to college and get good, high-paying jobs like you rich guys do. We have to work for a living—and work hard! I don't think you understand that. It seems to me that you look down your snooty nose at the rest of us. I find that very offensive. There! And I mean every word of it. Signed, Branson."

"Branson: Wow . . . I'm sorry you feel that way. I don't feel that way. I think I've been very lucky in my work life; however, I also believe that luck is a dividend of sweat. The more you sweat, the luckier you get. And, Branson, my friend, we don't have to agree on anything to be kind to one another."

"Noah: My wife and I like to go to movies—or, at least we used to like it. Nowadays, the language is so filthy it's embarrassing to listen to it. I don't know people in real life who talk like that, and I'm a member of the Teamsters union. Why does Hollywood think we normal people like hearing them curse every sentence? It's disgusting! Signed, Lawrence."

"Lawrence: I totally understand. Even the nicest people, like us, have our limits. But as for Hollywood . . . never underestimate the power of stupid people in large groups."

"Noah: My husband left me about eighteen months ago for a younger woman. It's hard getting over that. I had no idea anything was wrong between us. I feel so broken now—useless and incomplete. I don't feel like I have a normal life anymore. I never thought he could end up hurting anyone so badly, especially his own wife. I guess we never truly know people, do we? Signed, Still Hurting."

"Still Hurting: I am so sorry. I wish there was something I could say to make you feel better. And I know sometimes people think that all they want is just to disappear, but in reality, all they want is to be found. Write to me anytime for an encouraging word and know that we ALL are a little broken. And that's okay."

"Noah: I need some advice, but not from my parents. I have an opportunity to do something that scares me a little but it could be incredible. Do you think I should pursue it? Signed, Dale."

"Dale: Obviously, I'm not your parents, and you should always listen to what they have to say. However, if something is both terrifying and amazing, then I think you should definitely pursue it."

TWENTY-NINE

The hike on Saturday was one Noah had never been on before. He was hoping it didn't have a lot of uphill to it. He knew Duncan wouldn't be coming out today but he wasn't sure how many others would be joining him. He pulled in the parking lot and only saw two vehicles, one of which was probably the ranger's. As he was getting his backpack out, the older gentleman from the other hikes came from the offices followed by Dorothy, the ranger.

Noah asked about the hike today and Dorothy told him it was into an area called the Maze, which was new to Noah. They waited about fifteen minutes but no one else showed up, so they took off. As usual, the older guy fell in behind Dorothy and Noah was third in line, but still with a good view of her legs. And, as in previous weeks, after about an hour and a half, the older guy said, "Well, that's it for me. You guys enjoy the rest of the day." He abruptly turned around and headed back to his car. They were now used to his behavior so they each waved to him and kept on walking.

It was a warm day with not much shade. This particular hike was a circular route, not out and back as the others had been. They walked most of the morning, stopping only for a quick rest and some water. Finally, they came to an area where there was a small spring bubbling up from the rocks. Noah went over to it but Dorothy quickly warned him, "That water is not safe to drink. There's a little arsenic in it. Not enough to kill you, but it'll make you really sick."

The water had made a small pool about eight feet across and ten feet wide, with sparkling, clear water. It looked delicious. Noah looked at the pool, then back at Dorothy and asked, "Are you sure about the water? It looks great! All clear and clean . . . are you certain?"

"Trust me. If the water was good, there would be all sorts of little bugs and critters in it. When you see clear water like that, with nothing in it, there's a good reason—it's poison. But, if you want to test it and get sick and throw up, then be my guest."

Noah looked at her, then looked back at the water, and decided to drink from his water bottle instead. They sat there in a little shady spot that was just big enough for them both to sit in. In fact, their shoulders had to slightly touch for them both to be in the shade. Dorothy ate some granola, nuts, and raisins. Noah ate a Hershey bar that had mostly melted, a peanut butter sandwich, and an orange. A blue lizard ran back and forth in front of them chasing something they couldn't see.

As they were eating, a white-winged crossbill landed in the juniper tree in front of them. It kept squawking at them because they were probably too close to its nest. It finally quieted down but kept its eyes on them just to make sure. Noah finally broke the silence and asked Dorothy if she was looking forward to her date tonight with Duncan. It took Dorothy a moment or two to answer, but she finally said, "Yeah, I guess so. Are you dating anyone tonight?"

Noah thought that was an interesting question, but he answered truthfully, "No, I'm not. The girl I'd like to date doesn't live here."

Perfect, thought Dorothy, let me see what I can find out. "Where does she live?"

"North Carolina. I'm trying to talk her into visiting here soon."

"What's her name? If you don't mind me asking."

Noah seemed to perk up a little and answered, "Ana. It's a beautiful name, isn't it?"

"Yeah, I like it. Much better than Dorothy."

Noah quickly added, "That's not what I meant. Dorothy is okay, it's just that . . . "

"You don't have to explain anything; I understand. Ana is a great name. I like it."

Noah smiled at this and added, "Yeah, she's great. I really miss her."

"What does she look like?" Dorothy could hardly keep from smiling as she asked this.

Noah looked up at the little bird, then down towards the lizard and said, "Well . . . she's really pretty and very smart. We both like a lot of the same things and just seem to always be on the same wavelength."

Dorothy nodded and took a drink of water, then asked, "What color hair does she have? Is it long or short?" She was loving this!

Noah checked his fingernails, then scratched his face and said, "It's not long or short. She just keeps it sort of trimmed. She likes it that way."

"What color is it?"

Noah thought for a moment, then said, "It was a little darker, but it lightened during the summer. She stays outdoors a bit."

Dorothy looked over at him and asked, "What kind of work does she do?"

"She's a professional. She graduated from The College of the Ozarks, have you heard of that?"

Dorothy said, "Yeah, I think I have. How did you two meet?"

"That's an interesting story, actually. We were set up on a blind date by a mutual friend, and at first we didn't really like each other. We were both coming off relationships that left us both a little disappointed. I really didn't want to see her after that first date but my friend insisted. He said Ana really liked me. So eventually I gave in and called her and we've been together ever since."

Dorothy really got a kick out of this story since absolutely none of it was true. She asked, "How long have you two been dating?"

"Oh, it's been a while now. We're getting pretty serious. She really wants to quit her job and move out here with me, so we're just waiting for the right time."

"Wow, that's really great. I wish something like that would happen to me someday."

During this entire conversation, quite by circumstance and comfort, their shoulders leaned against each other a little more. In fact, their arms were lightly touching all the way down to their elbows. Neither one made an effort to move. They sat there, leaning against each other for probably fifteen more minutes before the little white-winged crossbill dove down at their feet in a futile attempt to snare the lizard. The sudden movement startled Noah and his hand involuntarily brushed against Dorothy's leg, just below the hem of her shorts. This short, involuntary reflex sent shivers up both their spines. Shivers in their spines, wild thoughts in their minds, and hormones raging throughout their bodies.

Sweat instantly popped out on Noah's brow as Dorothy said, "Well, I guess we'd better be heading back if we're going to make it before dark." Noah didn't want to head back. Neither did Dorothy. But they did.

All the way back on the trail, Noah kept looking at the spot on Dorothy's leg that he had inadvertently touched. Dorothy, too, kept looking down at her leg to the place Noah had inadvertently touched. In what seemed like five minutes, they were back at the parking lot. Several other tourists were milling about and another park ranger was closing up the offices as they walked in. He yelled over to Dorothy, "Hey, I was getting ready to send out a search party for you two. Whatcha been doing?"

Dorothy quickly yelled back, "We weren't doing anything. Nothing!" She looked over at Noah for confirmation and he also yelled back,

"Nothing at all."

The other ranger nodded. The other tourists smiled and they were all thinking . . . "Right."

Noah drove back towards Moab in a fog. He kept trying to think of Ana but all he could remember was touching Dorothy's leg. Dorothy drove back trying to think how she was going to make it through dinner tonight with Duncan, when all she could focus on was Noah's hand touching her leg. It's a good thing the road back to Moab is fairly straight with very little traffic. A good thing indeed.

THIRTY

Duncan was right on time as he knocked on Dorothy's door. She smiled and grabbed her purse as she set the alarm. She was wearing a skirt that was about three inches above her knees, a skirt that Duncan liked a lot. As she closed the door, Duncan took her hand and started walking her to his car—a move Dorothy was not expecting. As Dorothy sat down in Duncan's truck, she started wishing she had worn slacks instead of a skirt.

Then, the first piece of bad news for the evening—Duncan did not make reservations at the new steak restaurant and they were told the wait would be at least an hour and a half. They didn't want to wait, so they drove down the street to the Moab Brewery, which was always full, but at least they wouldn't have to wait. They spotted a table near the bar that hadn't been cleaned off yet, but they took it anyway and waited for the staff to come and clean it. Then, the second piece of bad news. As soon as they sat down, Dorothy looked up and saw Noah looking back at her from his stool at the bar.

Noah had come straight to the Brewery to think about his day on the trail and sort out his thoughts and feelings for Ana, as well as his thoughts and feelings for when he touched Dorothy's leg earlier today. Why had a stream of excitement filtered through his body? And, more importantly, why was it still there? As he was contemplating these issues, while munching on some sweet potato fries, he saw Dorothy and Duncan sitting at the table right in front of him.

When Duncan saw him, he yelled out, "Hey, buddy, come on over and sit with us."

Noah reacted quickly with a believable lie. "Sorry, I can't, I'm with some friends over there." He pointed mindlessly to the other side of the bar. He quickly picked up his pint, but left the fries, and went to the other side of the bar where he pretended to talk to some complete strangers.

Unfortunately for Noah and Dorothy, the bar stool where Noah now sat was directly facing Dorothy. He tried not to make eye contact with her. Instead, his eyes went below the table where he saw her cross her legs in that short skirt. Oh, my. He took one more healthy drink from his Black Raven Stout and decided he had to leave. Dorothy heard Duncan talking, but she wasn't paying attention to anything he said as she watched Noah exit the pub.

She had no idea what Duncan had said but she knew she could never make it through dinner with him. She looked at him and said, "Duncan, I'm sorry, but I need to go home. I think I got dehydrated on the hike today and I just don't feel good. I'm sorry."

When Duncan was talking earlier, as Dorothy wasn't paying attention, he told her how he really didn't like the pub when it was so crowded. He suggested they go back to her place for a drink. Then when Dorothy said she needed to go home, that was all he heard. He was ready! He drove them back to her place and cut the engine off, then scampered around to open the door for her. She was already out of the car by then, but he walked with her up to the front door, expecting great things inside. She said, "I'm so sorry, I just feel sick and need to go to bed early. Maybe some other time, okay?"

"Huh?" It just dawned on him what she was saying. She really didn't want to go inside and jump his bones? She didn't want to abuse his body or explore the unknown with him? She was sick?

"I'm sorry, Duncan. Please forgive me. I need to take something and go to bed." As she said this, Dorothy turned and stepped inside before Duncan could respond. He wondered what had just happened. He stood there hoping she might reconsider and open the door for him, but she didn't. After a few moments, he dejectedly skulked back to his truck—very disappointed and confused.

Dorothy went straight to her computer to see if there was an email from Noah waiting for her. There was not. But as she sat there thinking, she heard the ding from her inbox— an email from Noah.

"My dearest Ana, I miss you terribly. Is there any way you can come and visit me? Or, just tell me where you are and I'll come there. I really need to see you. Noah."

She wrote back, "Noah, I wish it was that simple, that I could just hop right over and visit you, but you know it's more complicated than that. I have thought about you all day and have been wondering what you did today. Please tell me, Ana." She wanted to know if he would say anything about the hike and the Ranger . . . or, anything. She also thought, I need to tell him, now, who I am. This has gone on long enough.

As Noah sat there thinking what to write next, his doorbell rang. He looked through the peephole and saw Duncan. He opened the door and Duncan started telling him what happened. "She got sick on me buddy. She said she got dehydrated today on the hike and felt terrible and needed to go home. She wanted me to come and lie down with her, but I didn't want to intrude."

"So, you took her home?"

Duncan nodded and continued, "Yeah, but not before she assaulted me on the front porch. She was all over me with her tongue halfway down my throat. That girl had it bad for me. I can only wonder what she'll be like when she's not sick."

Noah didn't know how he felt. Jealous? Mad? Surprised? Angry? Before he could figure out what to say, Duncan continued, "She hinted she would make it up to me big-time! Then she tried again to get me to come in with her, but if she was sick, then she needed to rest. So, I made her go in by herself but promised I'd make it up to her the next time."

"So, you're going to see her again?"

Duncan smiled and answered, "Buddy, the way that girl wants me, I'd be a fool to turn her down."

They drank a beer together before Duncan left. Then Noah went back to the computer. At least this visit from his friend helped him clarify his feelings a little better. He had totally misread the situation with the ranger. He wrote back to Ana, "I went on a long hike today. It was nice, but all I could think about was you, dear Ana."

"Who else went on the hike with you? Or, were you alone?"

"For the most part, it was just me and a ranger. I wish it had only been me, though. I don't think I want to go on any more hikes with her. I enjoy the solitude of my own self much more."

This made Ana curious. "The ranger wasn't unprofessional, was she?"

Noah didn't really want to continue this ranger conversation, so, only to the change the subject, he wrote, "No, she was fine. Just not for me. I'd much rather be alone."

When Ana read this, she started crying. She turned her computer off and cried more. She knew it all along . . . Noah was much too good for her.

Noah sat and sat and sat, waiting for a reply. But none came. He wrote a short message, but still nothing in reply. He didn't understand why. He also didn't understand why he couldn't stop thinking of Dorothy and the way he felt sitting next to her and the thrill he felt simply by accidentally touching her leg. For Noah and Ana both, it would be a long, difficult, restless night.

THIRTY-ONE

"Noah: This is hard to explain, but I think I'm too nice. It seems to me that all the girls want 'bad boys' and don't really care about nice guys. You get a lot of letters from women; what do they want? From what I can tell, they don't want guys like me. They only confirm that old adage: 'Nice guys finish last.' Signed, Nice Nick."

"Dear Mr. Nick: I don't know what women want. I wish I did! However, I DON'T believe nice guys finish last. Boring guys do."

"Noah: I read that here in Salt Lake City we are in the top 4% of educated people in the country. I also read that we have over three hundred sunny days a year here in Utah. And that 71% of Utahans have donated money to charity and 56% of us have volunteered our time to help others. This all makes me very proud. What do you think of these statistics? Signed, Proud & Beaming."

"Dear P&B: I also love Utah, but I've found that statistics are like a bikini . . . what they reveal is suggestive, but what they hide is vital."

"Noah: I know you have a problem with Mormonism; that's easy to see from your column. I just don't think you've researched it thoroughly. Don't you think something that many people have sacrificed their lives for is worth your consideration? Signed, Mr. T. T. Williams."

"Mr. T.T. Williams: Let me repeat, all I have ever done is question some of your beliefs—that's all. But let me also add this—a thing is not necessarily true because a man died for it."

<hr>

"Noah: What is the meaning of life? Signed, Margie."

"Margie: Unfortunately, just when I discovered the meaning of life, they changed it."

<hr>

"Noah: It's Hazel, I've written you several times and you always give me some glib answer. I don't think you love me like you love other people. Is that true?"

"Hazel: My dear, dear friend, I love you like a fat kid loves cake."

<hr>

"Noah: When are they going to pave 4th Street? Everyone else has good roads, so why can't we have good roads? Signed, Chuck."

"Chuck: Every storm runs out of rain . . . just be patient, dude."

<hr>

"Noah: Our new mayor hasn't made one good decision since he's been in office. Our state representative is worthless and our city council won't vote on anything worthwhile. It makes me upset to read about all the non-action going on around us. What do you think? Signed, Kenny."

"Kenny: If you're not happy, that's your fault. Every minute you're not dead should be a minute spent enjoying the heck out of life. That's what I think."

<hr>

"Noah: My nephew is just not being sensible. He's nearly thirty years old but won't take any responsibility for anything. He's never been married and all he does is party with his friends. I'd like to do something to help him but I just don't know what. His parents live in California and I feel an obligation to help him. Any suggestions? Signed, Gail."

"Gail: My dear, you cannot save people, you can only love them."

"Noah: If you only had two hours left on earth what would you do? Signed, Addison."

"Addison: I'd fall in love with as many things as possible."

"Noah: Why do I always get jury duty summons and my husband never gets one? Signed, Ruth."

"Ruth: Say this prayer with me: Lord, give me coffee to change the things I can change, and wine to accept the things I can't."

THIRTY-TWO

Dorothy went to work Monday morning and filled out reports, processed applications, analyzed spreadsheets, and answered questions and emails from her bosses in the Salt Lake City regional office. Not the type of work she envisioned when she signed up for the Park Service as a ranger. She thought about submitting an application for a job at Grand Canyon National Park, but quickly dismissed that idea—too many tourists and crowds. But how could she stay here? Moab was such a small little town that she'd be running into Noah all the time . . . she couldn't stand that.

She came to the decision that she would not answer any more of his emails. It was time to stop living this fantasy of hers and get on with her life, such as it was: broken-hearted, dejected, rejected, lost, and forlorn. At least she knew without a doubt that Noah did not want her. He'd told her that much in the email when he wrote that the ranger was, "Just not for me. I'd rather be alone." Those two short sentences ended Dorothy's dream and finished the fairytale of Ana and Noah. She would not answer any more of his emails and she would never write him again. This morning, before work, she sent her last message to him which simply read, "Noah, please don't write to me anymore. I'm changing my email address. Good luck and I'm sorry. Ana."

Noah was stunned when he read the email from Ana. He tried writing her, but it came back returned. That email address was no longer valid. He couldn't write to her, he couldn't call her, he couldn't visit her . . . wasn't even sure he could tie his shoes. He shouldn't have answered any work email questions this day, but he did.

"Noah: I think the city is going to annex some more property out near where I live. Do you know who I can contact to protest this? It's just not right they keep spreading out like this and forcing us to be in the city limits when we don't want to. Thanks. Signed, Candy."

"Candy: Sometimes life is going to hit you in the head with a brick. Don't lose faith. Or, you could always move to Las Vegas."

"Noah: I am a campaigner for social justice in our city and state. We are trying to right the wrongs of government and society and provide a decent level of living for all our citizens. We need to change the tax structure to enable more funds to be available to help the poor and unemployed and immigrants in our state. I feel certain you could help us by supporting this cause in your column. Can we count on your support, Noah? Signed, Samantha."

"Samantha: First, let me say this. My idea of social justice may be different from yours. My idea is that I keep what I earn and you keep what you earn. Do you agree? If not, then tell me how much of what I earn belongs to you—and why?"

"Noah: I'm in my second year of college. Apparently, I have two more years left to graduate unless I go to summer school, which I hate. I need summers off to recharge and have some fun. Are there any other shortcuts I can pursue to finish up quicker? Thanks, Furman."

"Furman: There are no shortcuts to anyplace worth going."

"Noah: We work to pay bills. We work to buy food. We work to get credit cards and pay more bills. We work to satisfy our needs and ego. I'm sick of work. How about you? Signed, Mikey."

"Mikey: Work is the curse of the drinking classes."

"Noah: There's this beautiful woman I see all the time at the gym. She never talks to anyone and always works out by herself. I'm wondering, does she work out alone because she's so pretty that all the other women are jealous of her? Or, because all the men are afraid to talk to her because she's so pretty and good? What do you think? Signed, Craig."

"Craig: I find it amazing how complete the delusion is that beauty equals goodness."

"Noah: I read in the paper that the Society of Justice, the Salt Lake City Bar Association, and the Utah Center for Equality and Progress are considering joining forces to better help those wronged by faulty court decisions. Do you think this will help? Signed, Dagmar."

"Dagmar: No, I don't. Lunatics never unite."

"Noah: I go the gym at least four times a week and have my own personal trainer. He works me hard and provides me with a protein diet and muscle supplements. I've been doing this for over six months but have yet to get as big as I think I should. I'm getting a little discouraged. Do you think I should stick with it or not? Signed, Will."

"Will: if size really mattered, the elephant would be king of the jungle."

"Noah: I have a question that seems crazy, but I'd like to know: If someone with a nose ring takes it out, then blows their nose, do they have to cover that hole as well as their nostril holes so the snot doesn't blow out everywhere? Signed, Just Wondering."

"Just Wondering: I'm going to answer that question with the shortest prayer in the Bible: "Lord, save me.""

"Noah: I'm in high school and we're studying wars and revolutions in Europe and South America. They both seem the same to me. What is the difference between a war and a revolution? Signed, Cynthia."

"Cynthia: War is when the government tells you who the enemy is. Revolution is when you figure it out for yourself."

"Noah: When I read the papers every day and watch the news at night, it worries me about what is happening to our country and the world. I mean, the economy, homelessness, global warming, the environment, and then add to that the fact that both political parties do nothing but blame each other. It worries the crap out of me. Does it worry you? Signed, Miles."

"My dear Miles: Worry is a misuse of your imagination."

"Noah: First of all, I'm old. Second of all, I'm opinionated. Third, I'm old but not stupid. From what I see, young people today are a bunch of lazy, selfish, worthless brats. Crying and complaining about everything. Always wanting somebody to give them something—I'd like to give them something! I know you won't print this, just as I know you younger people don't think like us older ones . . . it's a pity. Signed, Roscoe."

"Roscoe: You underestimate my thinking abilities. In my opinion, we're churning out a generation of poorly educated people with no skill, no ambition, no guidance, and no realistic expectations of what it means to go to work. I guess I'm old as well, Roscoe."

At this point Noah thought it best to stop for the day before he got himself in more trouble than normal. Usually, he tried to be more political in his answers, but this day was not normal. This day, he spoke without a filter; this day, all he wanted to do was go to the Moab Brewery and see how much he could actually drink before either dying, throwing up, or getting in a fight. And he wasn't choosy.

THIRTY-THREE

Noah pulled in the parking lot of the Moab Brewery but noticed Duncan's truck nearby. There was no way he could go in and possibly see Dorothy hanging all over Duncan right in front of him. He'd already lost Ana; there was no way he could fathom seeing Dorothy with someone else. As he pulled out of the parking lot he wondered to himself, "If Duncan hadn't come along and swooped her off her feet, would I have had a chance with her?" Then someone honked their horn at him as he absentmindedly crossed the center line. Oh well, what did it matter now? He started driving out to Castle Creek Winery; they were open late. Tonight, wine was better than beer.

As he was tasting wines at the bar area, his cell phone rang. It was Duncan. He started not to answer, but eventually, he couldn't help himself. "Hello."

"Hey, buddy, where are you? You coming to the Brewery tonight?"

Noah lied and answered, "Can't tonight, I've got a deadline I have to meet. I'll catch you later."

Knowing that Noah wasn't coming to the Brewery now, Duncan chose this opportunity to brag. "We'll miss you, buddy. Dorothy was just telling me about a friend of hers you might be interested in meeting."

"She's there with you?" Noah didn't really WANT to know, but he HAD to know.

Duncan took this opportunity to really pour on the lies. "Yeah, but the way she's clawing at me, we won't be here long—if you know what I mean."

Noah didn't want to know what he meant. Now, he wished he hadn't asked. His mind, absently, flashed back to that instant on the trail when his hand brushed against her leg, and he was silent.

"Hey, you still there?"

Noah broke from his reverence and replied, "Yeah, sorry, you two have fun. I need to get back to work. Bye." He hung up before he had to endure anymore. Then he gulped the last half glass of his wine in one big swallow. He spent the next two hours sampling every wine available. After his third glass, he didn't know if he was drinking dry wine, red wine, or motor oil. He didn't care. He just needed some way of getting the memory of Ana from his mind . . . and erasing the memory of an accidentally touched leg on the trail to nowhere.

Duncan called Dorothy repeatedly but she never answered any of his calls. She hoped he would soon give up and forget about her. She missed going to the little coffee shop on Main Street, but she just couldn't take the chance of running into Noah again. She even traded jobs with her fellow park ranger so she wouldn't be leading any hikes on the weekend. Duncan figured this out when he went there specifically to see Dorothy. When he found that she wasn't leading the hike, he turned around and went back home.

That weekend, Noah drove out towards Castle Creek to the end of a winding dirt road and decided to wander off toward the farthest butte. He didn't get far. Without marked trails walking in the wilderness was not a simple thing to do. Too many twists and turns and boulders and ledges to simply go from point A to point B. He finally gave up and just found a ledge he could sit on and stare into the abyss while thinking of all that had gone wrong.

He wondered why he fooled himself into thinking anything would ever happen with Ana. A woman who wouldn't tell him her name, or where she lived, or anything else about herself. He was so stupid. But, boy, it was a nice dream while it lasted. Her emails sent him into delusional states of euphoria. He wondered if he would ever meet anyone in real life who could make him feel that way again. He doubted it. He didn't wear a watch and soon lost complete track of time. He had no idea how long he'd been sitting here—dreaming.

After a few wrong turns, he finally made it back to the dirt road only to find a large, dust-covered, 4-door Chevy Silverado pulled in behind him, blocking the way. When he walked up to the vehicles, two large men opened the doors of the Silverado and stepped out to greet him. "This your Jeep here, dude?"

Noah said, "Well, it's not a Jeep, but it is mine. Something wrong?"

"Yeah, I'd say something's wrong. This here is a private road and you're on private property."

Noah didn't know that. He didn't know where he was. "Sorry, fellas, if you'll just back out of the way, I'll be moving on. Sorry for the inconvenience."

Neither of the men moved, except to spit on the ground in front of Noah. "Look, fellas, I don't want any trouble here. I'm sorry I trespassed on your land. I truly didn't know it was private. All I did was walk a little way in the desert and sit for a while."

The uglier of the two replied, "How do we know you didn't steal something?"

"Steal what? Rocks and dirt? There ain't nothing out there, fellas. You know that."

Neither of them answered, they just stared at him. Finally, the ugly one said, "Alright, git outta here and don't ever come back, you hear me?"

"Yeah, I hear you. No problem . . . I won't." They backed up a little and Noah turned around to leave. When he was pointed in the right direction, he gunned it and spun his back tires sending a plume of dust, dirt, and pebbles in the direction of the two guys who were still standing there watching him. Because of the cloud of dust, he couldn't see them, and he didn't wait around looking either. He drove as fast as could safely navigate the dirt road, all the way out to the highway. When he turned on the main road, he looked back but didn't see anything but his own dust tail in the sky. He absently thought, "I can't wait to get back and tell Ana what happened." Then, his smile quickly disappeared as reality jolted him back to his pitiful existence.

Noah was washing a load of clothes when his doorbell rang. He looked through the peephole to find Duncan smiling at him holding a six-pack of Coors Light. It was 10:30 in the morning; why is he bringing beer over here? As soon as he let him in, Duncan popped the top on one of the cans. Noah said, "Dude, it's not even noon yet."

Duncan smiled, wiped his mouth with his sleeve and answered, "It is on the east coast. Here, take one."

"No, I'll wait. I'm washing some clothes this morning, what are you up to?"

Duncan took another long pull and said, "I'm having woman problems. I need your advice."

Noah really didn't want to hear this, but he had little choice. "What sort of problems?"

"It's Dorothy. You remember her, right? The ranger?"

"Yeah, I remember her. What sort of problems?"

Duncan figured this was the best way to save face with Noah—lie about it. "She won't leave me alone. She's about to wear me out, man. Did you know she was a nymphomaniac? It's true! She told me. She wants me all night long, then early in the morning, lunchtime . . . I can't get any rest, man. I think I'm going to have to end it with her. We can't ever go out anywhere, that's why you never see us out at the Brewery. She's always demanding sex from me all night long. I'm telling you, she's wearing me out."

Noah said, "We're talking about the ranger who went on that hike with us, right?"

"Yeah, man. I'm gonna have to cut it off with her. There's more to life than sex every waking hour, you know what I mean?"

Noah had no idea what he meant. Couldn't even imagine it. He said, "That's just hard to believe. I would have never seen that in her. She looked so . . . innocent, I guess."

Duncan nodded and continued, "I guess we'll never figure 'em out, huh? You sure you don't want one of these?"

"No, I'm good, but thanks anyway."

Duncan smiled, happy that he'd explained why he was never seen with Dorothy, and why he would never be seen with her in the future. "Okay, I'll be running then. Maybe I'll catch up with you at the Brewery later."

Noah heard the buzzer on his dryer and started back to the laundry room, thinking, "Wow, that's hard to believe." He walked past his computer, stared at the blank screen and thought of happier times as he went to finish folding his clothes.

THIRTY-FOUR

"Noah: You answer questions all day, let me ask you this: What's your unanswerable question—the question you seem to always be asking yourself? Signed, Steve."

"Steve: That's a very serious question. Here's my answer: Where am I going, and why am I in this handbasket?"

"Noah: Some of my friends only watch CNN and other friends only watch FOX news. What is your assessment of each group? Signed, Robbie."

"Robbie: I think people who listen to and watch CNN and FOX deserve to be lied to."

"Noah: I really need to know the answer to this question: If a person owns a piece of land, do they own it all the way down to the core of the earth? Signed, Mo."

"Mo: Yes they do . . . unless they strike oil, natural gas, gold, coal, uranium, silver, or copper—then the government owns it. Plus, you cannot go past the center of the earth, because someone from China owns the other side. Finally, Mo, if you did dig a hole to the center of the earth and dropped a rock down that hole, did you know that it would take forty-five minutes for the rock to reach the bottom? Hope all this information has helped you, Mo."

"Noah: It seems to me that you are unhappy. Sometimes your comments are almost cruel. Are you happy, Noah? Signed, Jean."

"Jean: Yes, I'm always happy; sometimes I just forget."

"Noah: I need some advice. There are things going on in our community that just aren't right. Things that are morally wrong, if not legally wrong as well. I haven't said anything or done anything up to now, but I want to. Do you think I should keep my mouth shut or stir up the pot with my complaints? Signed, Lisa."

"Lisa: The world suffers a lot. Not because of the violence of bad people, but because of the silence of good people. God will not hold us guiltless. Not to speak is to speak. Not to act is to act. My advice, Lisa: Sometimes get carried away."

"Noah: There's this guy in my office who always wants to argue. He's just ornery and mean. It doesn't matter what the subject is, he'll argue with you just for the sake of arguing. It just ruins your day to talk with this jerk. What do you suggest? Signed, Norman."

"Norman: Never wrestle with pigs. You both get dirty but the pig likes it."

"Noah: I have graduated from college and have a nice job that I sort of enjoy. I really don't have any friends from work, though, and my high school friends have either moved away or gotten married. I seldom do anything but watch TV and visit my parents now. I used to have fun! I hope there's more to life than this. Signed, Bored to Death."

"Bored: Why do you stay in prison when the door is wide open?"

"Noah: All my friends have different ideas about you. We've never seen your picture but some of my girlfriends think you're probably good-looking. But some other girls think you must not be good-looking, or else, you would've put your picture in your column. Which is it, Noah? Signed, Carly."

"Carly: I am definitely ugly. I stuck my head out the window of my car and got arrested for mooning."

"Noah: I know people are always writing to you about their troubles and problems. I wanted to tell you that I don't have any of those issues. I don't know if there's anyone else like me, but I'm happy and healthy and thrilled to be alive. I have a good job, a great husband, a wonderful family, and an active and an enjoyable social life. So, Noah, hearing all this, do you think I have too much of a good thing? Signed, Connie."

"Connie: Your letter made my day. To answer your question, I think too much of a good thing can be wonderful. Keep on keeping on, Connie."

"Noah: From what I see, us humans are a pitiful lot. We're mean, selfish, hateful, rude, bigoted, deceitful, arrogant, and snobby. What sort of medicine can we all take to save ourselves? Signed, Mr. Pessimistic."

"Dear Mr. Pessimistic: The best medicine for humans is love. And if you find it's not working, increase the dosage."

"Noah: From what I gather, you never make any mistakes—is that right? You're always giving other people advice on what to do or what to say. I guess your life is perfect, huh? Signed, Chester."

"Chester: You have no idea, my friend. Sometimes even the Devil sits on my shoulder asking me, 'What the crap are you doing?'"

"Noah: My dad is in a nursing home and I visit him pretty regularly. He's still in good shape, and for that, we are blessed. However, many of the older people out there are bitter and somewhat mean at times. Not all of them, some are nice, but it is really surprising at the vast array of personalities—all around the same age. Have you heard this before? Signed, Ruby."

"Ruby: Good to hear that your dad is doing okay. Sounds like you're a good daughter—keep it up. Yes, I have heard this from others in your position. It seems as though some people age like wine while others age like milk. Getting old is never easy, Ruby. I visited an uncle at his retirement home once and I'll never forget what he told me: 'What a wonderful life I've had! I only wish I'd realized it sooner.' Don't we all?"

"Noah: I'm an English teacher at a high school here in Salt Lake City. I'm having my students study great poets of the past and pick out their favorite poems or phrases they have come across. I'm sure you have some favorite words that make you feel better, don't you? Can you share them with us? Signed, Mrs. Currie."

"Mrs. Currie: Yes, I do. My four most beautiful words in the English language are: I told you so."

"Noah: When I buy pain relievers there is always regular strength and extra strength. I wonder if there's any difference in them. Which one do you buy? Signed, Emily."

"Emily: Nobody wants a pain reliever that's anything less than extra strength. I always want the maximum allowable dosage. Figure out what will kill me, then back it off just a little bit."

THIRTY-FIVE

Dorothy spent her days doing paperwork and dreaming of past hikes. She went straight home from work most days. Once in a while she bought some groceries, nothing else. She watched television, she stared out her window at the distant LaSal Mountain Range. She would even sit at her computer desk and stare at the blank screen. She wouldn't turn on the computer because she didn't trust herself. She drank hot tea after work and wine before going to bed. She wondered if she should put in for a transfer and leave this God-forsaken desert and all the heartache with it. But she knew she couldn't.

Noah did all his work and answered questions from the good people of Salt Lake City. He thought about driving up there and visiting the office but decided against it. He checked his email account about four hundred times a day, which was an improvement from the thousand times a day he was checking it last week. He met Duncan a few times at the Moab Brewery, but Duncan had met a new beauty from a mountain-biking outfit in Moab. This new girl seemed to be a bit younger than Duncan and was easily impressed with his good job at the mining company. Soon, Noah was back to his old lonesome self at the Brewery, sitting there watching all the tourists laughing and drinking. Thinking about a girl he never knew and couldn't forget.

Noah had a vacation he had to take or else lose the days he had accumulated. He thought of going to North Carolina and searching its nearly six million residents for a girl he didn't know. He didn't think about it for long . . . but it did cross his mind. He wanted to get away from Moab, but not get away too far—he was a homeboy and he liked the comfort and feel he had grown accustomed to. Now that tourist season was winding down a little it would be easier to find some local adventure he could try out. He had always wanted to raft down the Colorado River, which runs right through Moab. This part of the mighty river has no rapids; it was mostly calm through the canyon country, only a few minor white-water sections that make it a little fun. A man could lean back in the raft and stare at the salmon-colored cliffs and peaks and dream the days away.

Noah knew several of the guides from the local outfitters and he waited to see one he could talk to at the Brewery. One night he saw a woman named Sandy come in by herself. She was nice and fairly good-looking, in a river running sort of way. Meaning that if you were on a week-long river trip, Sandy would start looking good about the fourth or fifth day out. She had that bubbly personality that all river guides must possess and it was easy talking with her. Noah bought her a beer and they sat as she told him some of the stories about the crazy things the tourists had done this season. It didn't surprise Noah; he'd heard them all before.

He asked her about any upcoming trips that he might be interested in. She told him of one they weren't advertising because it was just for some local friends of the company and they didn't want any tourists coming along to spoil everything. It would be two six-man rafts leaving from Moab and heading towards the old, forgotten, and drowned Glen Canyon. A place none of them had ever seen but all of them had read about. Noah signed up immediately to secure his spot on this magical trip. Once they set off from Moab, they wouldn't see another human being for the next one hundred and fifty river miles. Sandy gave him some information, verified the dates, and told him what to bring along. The tour company would provide almost everything in two additional floating rafts. Sandy told him just to bring his swimsuit—or not—that was completely up to him.

☾☾☾

Dorothy was in a deep funk. She missed her emails to and from Noah more than she ever imagined she would. Her life had a hole in it and she felt as though she was falling through that hole. Her boss at the Park Service noticed it as well. He knew something was bothering her and didn't want to intrude in her private life; however, he had a grand idea. All his staff needed to get experience in all aspects of the natural environment: nature trails, mountain climbing, backcountry adventures, and river running. He decided he would get his friends Lorraine and Sandy to take Dorothy with them on their next run down the Colorado. This would give her good experience and hopefully perk her up some. When he set it up and told her she'd be going on a week-long adventure down the Colorado, she just shrugged and said, "Okay."

As the trip drew near Dorothy finished up all her paperwork and paid some bills. If her boss hadn't insisted, she would never have done this on her own. Noah had a few questions to finish off for his column before his sabbatical, but he was really looking forward to getting away. Usually, once or twice a year, Noah would print all the crazier questions people had sent in . . . the ones that made very little sense or that were just unanswerable. He chose this week to publish a few of those:

"Noah: Aren't you tired of people asking you rhetorical questions and you don't know if they are rhetorical questions or not? Signed, Hank."

"Hank: You are reading my rhetorical mind."

"Noah: If a man is talking in the forest and there is no woman to hear him, is he still wrong? Signed, Clay."

"Clay: Take a wild guess."

"Noah: If nothing sticks to Teflon, how do they make Teflon stick to the pan? Signed, Myra."

"Myra: A wise man once said nothing."

"Noah: Why don't you take some writing lessons from Hemingway and Faulkner and Steinbeck, then maybe your column would be worth reading? Signed, Unsigned."

"Dear Unsigned: Eagles don't take flight lessons from chickens."

"Noah: I'm going to stop paying taxes! I don't care what they do to me, I just don't care, but I am not going to give another red cent to these lousy politicians. I think everyone should stop paying taxes—don't you? Signed, Mad Max."

"Max: Good idea. if you're going to be weird, be confident about it."

"Noah: My girlfriend was eating some ice cream when I got home and all I did was ask how she's doing. She flipped out! What is going on with women? Signed, Barney."

"Barney: You learned a valuable lesson . . . Never ask a woman who is eating ice cream straight from the carton how she's doing. Never!"

"Noah: Why is it that all men—ALL MEN—go straight to the woman with the big boobs? Signed, 32A"

"32A: Why? Because men can see better than they can think."

"Noah: I'm really mad. Signed, Buddy."

"Buddy: I totally understand."

Noah started to sign off for the week and close his computer, but first, he stared at the blank inbox on his emails hoping for a miracle. Nothing. As he stood there staring, almost as if by divine intervention, it dinged as an email appeared. Noah immediately thought, "Great. Another ad for erectile dysfunction or a bill." It was neither. It was an email from an unknown address with the heading "Ana." He knew all about spam and viruses and all the warnings about never opening anything from an unknown address . . . but this one said "Ana." He had no choice—he had to open it.

"Noah, I hope you'll forgive me for reacting so harshly and closing my email account. My life has been topsy-turvy lately. You have done nothing wrong. I feel so bad about how I overreacted that I had to try and apologize. I never intended to hurt you; however, circumstances arose that took me by surprise and I felt I had no options at the time. Please forgive me if you can. I truly miss our conversations and even though we may never meet in person, I would hate to know we could never communicate any longer. Can we still be friends? Please?

"If you will forgive me and let me have another chance at being your friend, I promise I'll always be here for you. Unfortunately, I have to go away for a week and I'll be out of touch—a family thing. As soon as I return, I'll let you know and we can begin where we left off. Is that okay? This email address is not mine, please don't respond to it. I'll give you my new address when I return. Noah . . . I miss you.

Always . . . your Ana"

Noah was stunned. He wanted to type a long letter of love to Ana, but he relented to her wishes and didn't write back. He would wait a week for her next email to him. After all, he was going to be away as well on his river trip. Except that now he would be the happiest man on the river, knowing that his Ana would be waiting for him when he returned.

ɷɷɷ

Dorothy couldn't help herself. She could not exist without Noah in her life; even knowing that it would only be through email, at least it would be something. She was pretty sure if she didn't get Noah back in her life that she'd never make it back alive from her river trip.

THIRTY-SIX

Noah arrived at the river early that first morning. Sandy and a few others were loading up the two supply rafts with food and beverages. There would be twelve total people in two rafts, plus the two supply rafts. The rafts were big and sturdy enough to probably hold ten or twelve people, but this trip was just for friends and for having fun and relaxing. Noah helped carry supplies from the Jeeps to the rafts, the supplies consisting of at least half wines and beers. There was also a nice grill and other essentials but no suitcases. Noah knew beforehand to only carry what would fit in a small waterproof backpack: Swimsuits, shorts, and tee shirts would be all they would need, plus sunscreen and a toothbrush. Also, no cell phones were allowed, since there would be no service this far out in the wilderness anyway. Sandy brought a short-wave radio in case of emergencies.

Dorothy woke up on the day of the trip and tried her best to talk herself out of going. Not that she didn't think it would be fun, but because she desperately wanted to start her email conversations with Noah again. She waited until the last minute then threw a swimsuit, shorts, and a couple of tee shirts into her pack and started for the door. She started to apply a little makeup but thought, "What's the point?" She'd be out on the river with people she knew and didn't need to impress any of them. She hadn't even shaved her legs in a few days . . . so what?

Dorothy was the last person to arrive as the others were tying things down in the rafts and making final preparations. She parked and started walking over to the river's edge saying hello to everyone: "Hey, Sandy . . . Craig . . . Joe . . . Dale . . . Bill." Suddenly she was paralyzed. She stared straight at Noah as he was staring straight back at her. First, she thought, "Is this real?" Then she thought, "I've got to get out of here."

But before she could decide which was more appropriate, he called out to her, "Hey, Dorothy, over here. You're in our raft."

She started stumbling towards the raft where Noah was and thought, "You don't have on any makeup, you didn't brush your hair, and you stupid girl, you didn't even shave your legs! Idiot!!"

Noah took her pack and threw it in the back and said, "Looks like you just woke up there, Ranger."

Dorothy was so embarrassed that she didn't respond; she just stepped into the raft and sat near the rear, waiting for the others to climb in. Craig, Joe, Sandy, Dale, and Noah were in the raft with her. She knew them all and they were all good people--fun to be with . . . all except Noah. How did this happen? There was one oar stowed in the back but the current was strong enough that no rowing was needed on the Colorado. A rudder would keep them centered in the main river channel. All they had to do was sit back, look at the salmon-colored cliffs, tell jokes and lies, and enjoy the company. Dorothy wanted to get out and go home.

Sandy sat at the very back so she could handle the rudder, the others lined up on each side. Noah ended up diagonally across from Dorothy so that their legs extended next to each other. She saw Noah looking at her unshaved legs and instantly became very embarrassed and self-conscious. As soon as they were in the main current, Sandy said, "Hey, Dorothy, have you and Noah ever met?"

Noah answered that question for her: "Yeah, we've been on a few hikes together and she dated one of my friends for a while."

Dorothy immediately replied, "Dated one of your friends? What are you talking about?"

"Duncan. You two dated several weeks ago, didn't you?"

Dorothy was flabbergasted! She said, "We went to dinner one time and didn't even eat anything. I got sick and went home before we ordered and I never saw him again. He called me a few times but it never worked out and I never saw him again. I don't call that 'dating' anyone . . . do you?"

Noah should have known to never believe anything Duncan said about women. He didn't know how to respond to Dorothy, but everyone in the raft was looking at him waiting for an answer. He finally said, "I'm sorry . . . I totally misunderstood what he said."

Before he could make things worse, Sandy jumped in and said, "Hey, we all know Duncan, you can't believe anything he says. He once told my best friend that he and I were engaged because we drank a Bud out of the same bottle." Everyone laughed . . . except for Dorothy. She wanted to jump over the side and swim back home--against the current.

The rest of the morning was quiet as they gazed, snoozed, and felt the strength and might of the river below them, nothing separating its might from them except a thin layer of rubber. Dorothy pulled her floppy, wide-brimmed hat down over her face as far as she could so that Noah couldn't see her face and so that she wouldn't have to look at him. She was still embarrassed by her unshaven legs and make-up deprived face. Noah pulled his ball cap down just far enough over his eyes so that Dorothy couldn't see him staring at her legs. He didn't notice that her legs hadn't been shaved or that she didn't have on any makeup. He was thinking about how nice her legs were. He thought it must be the hiking that helped shape them so nicely. Then he thought of that lying Duncan telling him that Dorothy was a sex maniac. He should have known better than to believe anything Duncan told him.

Noah dozed off and was jolted back awake as the rafts bumped against the shore. Sandy spotted a place with a small beach area under some tamarisk trees, and she steered the rafts over for lunch and bathroom breaks. As usual on river trips, the women went upstream and the men went downstream. As they were walking back to the rafts, Sandy asked Dorothy about Noah: Dorothy answered, "He went on a couple of guided-hikes with me out at Canyonlands. It was always with a group of tourists and I barely remembered his name."

Sandy nodded and answered, "Well, he remembered your name alright but he must've forgotten what your legs look like because he's been staring at them all morning."

Dorothy's face instantly flushed and she said, "He was not! He was asleep most of the time. You're crazy!"

Sandy just smiled and said, "Right, you keep on believing that, girl."

The afternoon rolled on lazily, effortlessly, wistfully . . . each person in their own dreams and thoughts. Some ruminated on past lovers, others contemplated future lovers, whereas some only stared at the cliffs and wondered if a man could lose his soul or his mind wandering through the endless maze of canyons on each side of the river. The shoreline wasn't large enough for anything but a few tamarisk trees and maybe some cactus to grow very sparingly. Most of the time the canyon walls came straight down into the river. The only wildlife they saw were a few lonely vultures floating on the thermals high above them.

Noah sat close to the edge and dropped his hand into the water as they drifted along occasionally dreaming of Ana and how their relationship would evolve now, but more often, stealing glances at Dorothy's legs and her face when she wasn't looking. Dorothy finally relaxed and stopped worrying so much about her lack of make-up and her unshaven legs. Each time she would turn to look at a passing cliff, she would quickly glance at Noah to see if he was looking at her. Nearly every time she did this, their eyes would meet for a half second—but that's all it took to confirm what they already knew.

The expedition found a suitable stopping point for the night: a sandy beach with a few trees and some broken limbs to start a campfire with. The guys all set up tents and arranged sleeping bags while the women started up the grill and prepared the dinner. Dale tried his luck at fishing in the river, which was mostly a futile effort. He'd heard there were rainbow trout and large-mouthed bass in the river but he never even got the slightest nibble. It was hot dogs and potato chips for everyone tonight, with your choice of boiled river water, local wine from Castle Creek Winery, or watered-down beer from the Rockies.

As the sun set below the canyon rim, the weather cooled considerably and everyone put on a light jacket as they sat around the campfire. A few stale jokes were told, old friends were remembered, and tales of mystery and intrigue on the river were recanted. No one knew if these tales were true or not, but as darkness set in, they seemed more real. Since there was no chance of rain this time of year, Noah decided to pull his sleeping bag under a small tree and sleep in the open instead of in a tent. All of the girls paired up and found tents, as did all the other guys. Noah wanted to be alone and think. Think of what? Ana, his column, Ana, his life, Ana, the ranger, Ana, Dorothy's legs, Ana, Dorothy's face, Dorothy's legs again, Dorothy's voice, and . . . oh, yes . . . Ana.

THIRTY-SEVEN

A bright, beautiful morning and they were on the river again. After about an hour and a half, they spotted a side canyon with a small stream spilling into the river. This particular stream wasn't on the map that Sandy had so they decided to paddle over and explore it. Two of the guys decided to stay with the rafts and relax while Noah, Dorothy, and the others started up the little stream. The underbrush was a thick tangle of scrub oak, tamarisk, and unknown bushes which made progress slow and uncomfortable. Then, almost as if by magic, the small canyon opened up into a pool of crystal-clear water, which seemed to be about four or five feet deep. The pool stretched from one canyon wall to the other, about fifteen feet, which made further progress impossible, except through the pool.

Four of the guys and Sandy wanted to swim through the pool and explore the other side, which seemed like a good idea to Noah as well. Then one of the guys said, "We need to take our clothes off so they don't get wet. Is everyone okay with that?" All the other guys immediately agreed, as did Sandy, whose sexual orientation seemed to be apropos to who she was with at the time. Dorothy hadn't agreed to go but Noah had. The other guys and Sandy started shedding clothes quickly . . . Noah never moved. Finally, one of the guys yelled at him, "Are you coming?"

Noah looked quickly over at Dorothy, who said, "Go ahead. You'll like it, it'll be fun." It wasn't really the fun part Noah was thinking about. The pool of water was still rather cool, and Noah knew what cool water could do to a man's manhood—and Dorothy was watching! The other guys started yelling at him to hurry up and strip. He walked to the edge of the pool, turned his back to Dorothy, quickly stripped, then jumped in the water. It almost took his breath away it was so cold. He beat all the others to the far side of the pool, then climbed out and ran into the jumble of bushes and trees down the trail.

Dorothy laughed at his actions but knew he would eventually have to come back through the bushes and into the pool . . . and she would be waiting. Some forty-five minutes later, Dorothy heard their voices on the trail back. She jumped up and stood on the edge of the water, next to where Noah had left his clothes. Noah had positioned himself behind one of the guys as they walked up to the pool, and then followed him into the water. When they made it to the other side where Dorothy was standing, Noah stopped, waist deep in the water, and said to Dorothy, "Can you hand me my shorts please?"

Dorothy answered, "Don't you want to get out of the water first?"

"No, I'm fine. Just hand them to me."

Dorothy grinned and replied, "You should get out and dry off first."

Noah said, "I didn't bring a towel."

Dorothy nodded but didn't say anything. Noah looked up at her and said, "Well?"

Dorothy leaned over and grabbed his shorts and held them out to him. Noah was still about five or six feet from the edge and couldn't reach them without exposing himself. He asked, "Can you just throw them to me, please?"

"I'm not a very good thrower. Why don't you just step out and get them."

Noah was flustered, and said, "Why don't you just step in and bring them to me?"

Immediately, Dorothy took her shirt off, took her bra off, took her shorts and panties off, and waded into the water and handed Noah his shorts. She then turned around and walked back out of the pool. Sandy watched all this happen, then said, "Alright, Noah, close your mouth and quit drooling, then get out of the pool. We need to get moving."

Back in the raft again, Noah and Dorothy took their spots but didn't speak to each other as they pushed off from shore. Secretly, Dorothy thought, "I hope he liked that."

Noah was thinking, "Dang!"

ᘓᘓᘓ

Their camp that night was on a sand bar in the middle of the river. There were several scrubby trees that provided enough broken limbs and branches for a nice fire pit and grill. After a dinner of hamburgers and roasted potatoes, the girls all had wine and the guys all had beer—funny how that works. As the sun dipped below the cliffs, before it was totally dark, the ladies went on one side of the sandbar and the guys went on the other to take a quick dip in the water and wash as best they could. Inhibitions were quickly, or slowly, depending on the point of view, disappearing.

For Noah, sleep came in fits that night. He thought he kept hearing noises in the trees, then in the water; however, it may have been the lasting memory of Dorothy walking to him, nude, in the little pool that was making his mind quiver. Dorothy had no trouble sleeping. The wine seemed to ease any tensions she may have been harboring about disrobing in front of Noah earlier. She didn't regret doing that and hoped he didn't regret seeing her do that.

The next day the river broadened out and gave them some views of rolling hills in the distance. They also saw a few deer on the banks and several cattle grazing in the scrubby fields. It was a lazy day on the Colorado and no one minded. Noah and Dorothy talked about their favorite books and some of their favorite nature trails around Moab as they floated along. Their conversations were becoming more comfortable with each passing day.

That evening, after they stopped and pitched their tents, Sandy, Noah, and Dorothy walked up a slight incline where they could see the countryside. As they sat on a boulder to contemplate the view, they heard someone from the camp shouting Sandy's name. She rolled her eyes and rose to walk back toward the rafts, leaving Noah and Dorothy sitting side-by-side, close together. When Sandy left, Dorothy, who was sitting in the middle, could have scooted over a little . . . but she didn't. They had become so comfortable with each other that they didn't need to force a conversation, so they sat there silently and delightfully contented.

Before it became totally dark, they made their way back to the camp and sat around the fire with the others. Dale told a few X-rated jokes. Sandy told about her first lesbian experience. Craig retold his story of getting lost in the Rockies and almost starving—which they'd all heard several times before but he always added new facts or fables to the tale to keep it interesting. Dorothy sipped her wine and wondered about Noah. Noah sipped his beer and watched the flickering light of the campfire bounce off Dorothy's legs. Neither of them wanted the river trip to end.

After a breakfast of granola bars, oatmeal, and bagels, the rafts pushed off again into the unknown—unknown to them. They experienced a small white-water section that got everyone's blood pumping pretty good, and they also witnessed a cormorant diving into the river ahead of them and coming out with a fish in its beak. They were back in the canyon country now and the walls came down into the river allowing virtually no shoreline at all. Fortunately, they found a small alcove up ahead which allowed them to pull over and take a short bathroom break.

When they boarded the rafts again, Joe changed places and sat in the raft with Noah and Dorothy. Noah thought nothing of it at first, but he had forgotten that Joe was also friends with Duncan. Duncan hadn't told Joe anything about his so-called date with Dorothy, because there was nothing to tell, but he had told him about Noah's fascination with a mystery woman via email. Now, Joe wanted to hear, firsthand, the story of Noah's lovesick confessions of a woman he'd never met or seen.

THIRTY-EIGHT

Joe plopped down next to Dorothy so he could be directly across the raft from Noah and so he could get a good look at Dorothy's legs. After they had all settled down and the current had them moving at a leisurely pace, Joe started his inquiry. "So, Noah, Duncan told me about your email girlfriend. Exactly how does that work?"

Noah was shocked! He didn't know how to respond or even if he should respond. Mostly, he didn't want to discuss Ana in front of Dorothy, or with anyone, for that matter. When Noah took too long to answer, Joe continued, "He says you don't even know her name. How do you talk to her if you don't know her name?"

Dorothy was initially shocked by this conversation, but since it directly concerned her, she gave it her full attention and stopped munching on some celery sticks she had. Noah's mouth opened as if he was going to say something, but no words came out. So, escalating his inquisition, Joe continued, "And he said you've never met her and you don't know where she lives. Is that right?" At this point, all the other passengers in the raft were now staring at Noah waiting to hear his reply. Dorothy was extremely interested to see how Noah would answer this.

Noah looked around the raft and saw everyone waiting on him to say something. Then he looked straight into Dorothy's face and she arched her eyebrows as if to say, "Well?"

"It's not exactly like that, Joe. You know how Duncan exaggerates everything—you can't believe anything he says."

Joe nodded, then asked, "Yeah, I understand. So, tell us exactly what we can believe. What's the mystery woman's name and what does she look like and where does she live?"

Noah wanted to jump overboard. Instead, as calmly as he could, he began his story, "We met online and her name is Ana. So, you see, Duncan was wrong about everything. She lives in North Carolina and has dark hair and went to school at The College of the Ozarks. She's my age, she has a professional job, and she's single—not married. There! Does that sound like I don't know anything about her?"

That answer shut Joe up but then Sandy asked, "Have you ever met her?"

Noah looked at Dorothy again before answering and replied, "Not yet. We just met a short time ago but she's planning a trip out here on her vacation."

Now it was Dorothy's turn to get in on the action, she asked, "Well, is it true that you're in love with her?"

No one had yet mentioned "being in love," and Noah wondered why she had asked that. Before he could answer, Joe jumped in and said, "Yeah, Duncan said you'd fallen off the deep end for this girl."

As he was trying to figure a way out of this, Sandy asked, "Is that true, Noah? You've fallen in love with a girl you met online?"

Noah thought, "Lord, please help me." And the Lord did. At that moment, the other raft hit a submerged rock in the river and sprung a leak. Air was hissing out as they all paddled furiously over to the river's edge. Apparently, a sharp-edged rock had punctured a hole in the bottom of the raft. They made it safely to shore and unloaded the damaged raft to find a two-inch slit in the rubber bottom. Fortunately, they had an emergency kit and quickly applied a patch to seal the raft. One of the guys took it out for a test to ensure its safety, then they brought it back and repacked everything to continue the journey. Noah was hoping Joe would get in the other raft. He didn't, but all the focus now was of the puncture and being on the lookout for submerged rocks. Joe took the lead and went to the front to keep an eye out for further danger.

Everyone else sat back and resumed their thoughts of life and rivers and canyons . . . all except Dorothy. She stared straight at Noah and when he looked at her, she arched her eyebrows again— but said nothing.

୦୦୦

At the end of the day, they found a nice sandy beach area to camp in and set up the tents. Noah stayed away from Joe and went off by himself to explore a small side canyon while the others did chores around the camp. At the head of the small canyon, he climbed up a few boulders and sat looking back over the river contemplating the day's events. Was he really in love with a phantom woman of unknown origin? Was he acting crazy over a woman who was virtually nameless and faceless to him? Was he falling for Dorothy? No . . . that part couldn't happen. It was the river, which had been known to drive men crazy in the past. This part could be explained. What couldn't be explained was how he felt about Ana.

Everyone enjoyed a beer or two around the fire that evening. Sandy grilled some sort of pork and some beef tips they had left in the cooler. The remainder of the trip would be meatless. Once again, after dinner, Noah pulled his sleeping bag away from the tents and chose to be alone and reflect on the river, Ana, and Dorothy, by himself under the stars and the moon, on the banks of the Colorado River, one hundred miles from the nearest town.

The next day was spent in wonder and fascination at the various colors and hues of the sandstone walls as they swept down the river. Every turn in the river now brought scenery they had never imagined. Apparently, the images from the river had swept aside any questions of Noah's email dalliances. He was happy to let that subject slither away. Another day, another night, another campfire, another imaginably spectacular day. Noah continued to sneak glances at Dorothy's legs and enjoy her smile when someone told a joke. She continued to pretend she didn't notice him staring at her legs, as she wondered if Noah was actually beginning to like the way she looked. She couldn't be sure. She also knew being on the river could make men act differently than they would back in civilization. Being out several days on the river could make even the mousiest of women seem glamorous and alluring to men. It had that effect.

The next to last night of their adventure was approaching and everyone could sense a foreboding of the end in sight. If it was up to them, they'd keep on going straight through Lake Powell, Lake Mead, and down the river all the way to Mexico. But they couldn't because of the dams around the lakes and irrigation and politics— all of which drained the mighty Colorado and turned it into a dry, dusty stream bed in lower Arizona. Plus, the fact they all had to get back to work next Monday.

That particular night found Noah and Dorothy sitting next to each other around the campfire. Dorothy had a glass of wine and Noah had a watery Rocky Mountain brew, as they sat and watched the fire flicker and pop at the river's edge. They were enjoying the company of each other, both wondering . . . about everything. One by one, all the others said their goodnights and went off to their tents. Dorothy and Noah stayed and enjoyed the solitude. Noah added a few broken limbs to the fire and poked it really good. Dorothy took small sips of her wine and listened to the river as it bounced off the sandstone walls.

Noah wasn't thinking anything except for how nice this was. Dorothy was questioning whether she should ask Noah some more things about the mysterious Ana. It would probably be her last chance to understand how he felt. She couldn't lose this opportunity, so she asked him, "Noah, tell me about your online friend, Ana. I'd really like to know about her."

He paused for a moment, took a sip of his beer and said, "Okay, if you truly want to hear it, I'll tell you."

"I do."

He started, "As I said, we met online through my work. It is true that I don't know her real name; she goes by Ana, which is fine with me—I like that name. It's also true I've never seen her and I don't really know where she lives. It's hard to understand . . . but none of that stuff matters to me. It's talking to her that's important. We think alike, we feel things alike, we want the same things. I'm afraid if I ever do meet her, I'll ask her to marry me at first sight!" He looked at Dorothy, who remained silent and motionless – after all, he was talking about her.

He continued, "She's really everything I ever dreamed of in a woman. Every day, all I look forward to is reading her emails, writing to her, thinking about her . . . but how do I explain that to other people? I can't really explain it to myself."

Dorothy asked him, "And you say you have no idea what she looks like? Wouldn't that make a difference to you?"

Noah answered, "I don't think so. Maybe. I don't know, but I don't think so. All I know is that I haven't seen any other woman that affects me like the thought of Ana does."

This was not really what Dorothy wanted to hear. It meant that her appearance isn't what Noah was looking for—just as she had always known—and dreaded from the beginning. But she kept silent. Secretly, Noah was thinking, "But if she looked like you, Dorothy, I'd elope with her right now!" But he also kept silent.

After a few quiet moments, Noah added, "She's just so honest with me. She tells me the truth about everything. I can always trust what she says. That may be the most important thing between us . . . trust."

Dorothy really didn't want to hear that either. She had been the opposite of honest with him. She drank the last half of her wine in one swallow, then said, "Thanks for sharing that with me, Noah. I appreciate it. I'm going to bed now. Goodnight."

Noah watched her walk away, thinking, "When I finally do meet Ana, I hope she walks like that."

THIRTY-NINE

The last day of the river trip was fairly uneventful. The last night was not. After dinner, everyone sat around a large fire they had made from driftwood and proceeded to finish off the wine and beer supplies. Things were fairly normal until the sun went down and someone shouted out, "Skinny dipping!" At that point, everyone except Noah stripped down immediately and jumped in the river. Then, after seeing Dorothy disrobe and jump in, he followed suit. There was drinking, dunking, and laughing going on above the water, and "other stuff" going on under the water.

By this time everyone was, as they say, "feeling no pain." Noah couldn't get too close to Dorothy because Joe, Craig, Dale, and Bill had her surrounded—in a friendly, platonic sort of way . . . sort of. Noah was envious, in a non-platonic way. As he was staring at the little group surrounding Dorothy, someone jumped on his back and threw their arms around his neck. He was hoping this person was a female. It was Sandy. She held him tight and said, "Are you having fun, Noah?"

Before he could answer, she let go of him and instantly swung around in front of him and kissed him deep and hard, while wrapping one of her legs around his torso (under the water). Noah had no decision in this sexual contortion . . . it was completely at Sandy's discretion, and she wasn't letting up. Noah moved a little to his left so he could see Dorothy's little group around Sandy's head, and as he did, he saw Dorothy looking directly back at him with Sandy's tongue in his mouth and her naked boobs pressed against his body.

Dorothy quickly excused herself from the group and waded ashore, as all the guys took in the scenery. As Noah was looking at her gather her clothes and walk away toward the tents, Sandy pulled away from him suddenly and wretched, then puked into the river. Obviously, she and the wine she'd been consuming had a major misunderstanding. Noah got her to the shore and the others quickly followed. Everyone dressed and tried to get Sandy dressed but she was heaving so badly they just covered her up and tried to comfort her.

Several minutes later, they were finally able to carry Sandy to her tent—still naked and passed out. All the guys went back to sit around the fire for a few minutes. Dorothy never appeared again. A few moments silently passed, then Dale said to Noah, "Dude, I've never seen Sandy kiss a man like that."

Noah replied, "I'm not really sure she knew I was a man."

Everyone laughed. Then everyone took one final drink and went off to their tents. Everyone except Noah. He sat there thinking of the vision of Dorothy walking nude out of the river. He wanted to savor that moment as long as possible.

❦❦❦

The last morning, several of the group had hangovers—none more so than Sandy. The bad news for them all was that no one had any Excedrin or Aleve's left. The good news was that they only had two hours of river travel to the take-out point. As they packed up everything and entered the rafts for the last time, Dorothy got in the other raft, leaving Noah, Joe, Dale, and the migraine-suffering Sandy alone in theirs. Accident or purposeful? Noah didn't know.

Hugs and handshakes all around (except for Noah and Dorothy). Promises of "Let's do it again soon," and "Call me," and finally, "See you at the Brewery." Dorothy quickly exited and drove away. Noah helped unload everything and take care of the rafts. Poor Sandy could only sit at a picnic table under a cottonwood tree and hope her head would soon quit hurting.

Noah finally made it home and went through a week's worth of junk mail and bills as he waited for his computer to fire up so he could see if Ana had emailed him. She had not. But she had told him she would be gone for a week visiting family. He was anxious to hear from her. He checked his work emails and had nearly two hundred questions from his readers in Salt Lake City, all waiting on some more words of wisdom from the all-knowing Noah.

He washed some clothes, prioritized his work emails, and checked the computer every five minutes for a message from Ana. Dorothy also washed some clothes and checked her mail and emails, wondering if she should continue with her dreams of Noah. Now, she knew for a fact that he was definitely in love with the phantom Ana, and just as definitely, had no desire for her-- Dorothy. She laid on the bed and cried. What's a girl supposed to do now? She had no idea.

FORTY

Noah sat down to catch up on his backlog of questions, always keeping an eye on his incoming email.

"Noah: What's the best way to get acid stains out of my blue jeans? Signed, Ricky."

"Ricky: Dude . . . don't try to get the stains out at all. Tell everyone you paid $110 to have them made like that. You'll be famous!"

"Noah: I don't like the way our culture is becoming so intolerant. I think we need to be more understanding and more progressive in our attitudes. Accept differences and embrace change. I'm sure you agree with this approach, don't you? Signed, Gwyn."

"Gwyn: My dear, in my humble opinion, tolerance is the last virtue of a dying society."

"Noah: I've been reading your column every day for a long time now. I've never written to you because I think that you think you're too smart and clever for us normal people. I might be wrong but I don't think so. Do you think you're more sophisticated and complex than us, Noah? Signed, Wanda."

"Wanda: To be perfectly honest, I'm so clever that sometimes I don't understand a single word of what I'm saying."

"Noah: I haven't read anything about your drinking exploits lately. Do all your friends drink like you? And what type of people would want to do that anyway? Signed, Ronald."

"Ronny: I think there are two types of people in the world: People you want to drink with, and people who make you want to drink. Cheers!"

"Noah: I need some advice. I want to save a bunch of money so I can retire early. I don't waste money in bars or clubs, I don't go to movies, I don't go out to eat very often—I'm doing all the right things that I can think of. Do you have any sage advice to help me? Signed, Linwood."

"Linwood: Nothing saves money like being antisocial."

"Noah: I have two girlfriends who I thought were my best friends. I've recently learned that they have been talking about me behind my back. It really hurt my feelings. I thought they were true friends that I could depend on. It makes me wonder . . . is there even such a thing as a true friend? Signed, Kate."

"Dearest Kate: I have found that 'true friends' don't judge each other; they judge other people . . . together."

"Noah: I love my husband but sometimes he is just crazy. He won't change the oil in his car because he doesn't think it helps. He won't exercise because he's lazy. He doesn't like anything on TV except old movies, and he won't get a computer or even a cell phone. He doesn't even think men actually walked on the moon—he thinks it's a hoax. He's a good guy, Noah, but I don't know what I can do to change him. Signed, Callie."

"Callie: Is that your real name? Anyway, to answer your question, we're all born ignorant, but one must work really hard to remain stupid. Sounds like your husband is a very hard worker."

"Noah: My son graduated from college about two years ago but still hasn't found a decent job. He's working and supporting himself at menial labor, while still taking courses at the college, but I think he needs to get going with his life. If not, he'll get left behind. What can I do to motivate him to get on the ball and start moving? Signed, Stewart."

"Stewart: I think direction is much more important than speed. Many people are going nowhere fast!"

"Noah: What's your favorite TV show? Do you like mysteries, comedies, or do you like the educational stuff? Signed, Grady."

"Grady: I find television very educational. Every time somebody turns on the set, I go into the other room and read a book."

"Noah: Why do you have to be so different? Signed, Arnold."

"Arnold: Different doesn't mean wrong."

"Noah: My husband and I just got back from visiting Alaska. It's beautiful up there, by the way. When we got back home we attended a conference on global warming and it concerned us very much. What is your newspaper's official view on 'global warming' and what is your personal view on this subject? Signed, Glenda."

"Glenda: To get the newspaper's official views, you'll need to write to the editor. All I can do is give you my personal opinion. My problem is I don't know much about global warming, so I did some research and I found this article published in the Washington Post, as reported by the Associated Press. It's from the Commerce Department from the Consulate in Bergen, Norway. It reports that the Arctic Ocean is warming up, that icebergs are growing scarcer, and in some places the seals are finding the water too hot. It reports that fishermen, seal hunters, and explorers all point to a radical change in climate conditions and hitherto unheard-of temperatures in the Arctic zone.

"Exploration expeditions report that scarcely any ice has been met as far as 81 degrees north and that the Gulf Stream is still very warm. Great masses of ice have been replaced by moraines of earth and stones, while at many points, well-known glaciers have simply disappeared. Very few seals and no white fish are found in the eastern Arctic, and within a few years it is predicted that due to the ice melt the sea will rise and make most coastal cities uninhabitable.

"Doesn't sound very good does it, Glenda? But before you get too concerned, I must mention that this article in the Washington Post was published on November 2, 1922. Glenda, do your own research, come to your own conclusions, and don't believe everything you read or hear from both sides of this argument."

"Noah: Please help me understand this question: If I were to rob a bank here in Salt Lake City, then drive to a sanctuary city in California, like San Francisco, could they arrest me there? Or, because it's a sanctuary city, would I be safe? Signed, Anxiously waiting for your answer."

"Dear Anxiously: I'm sure your friends love you anyway."

"Noah: I am so proud of my son that I just want to tell everyone how great he is. He graduated medical school and works in a hospital that specializes in helping the poor and homeless. I call him every week and tell him how proud I am of him. He's a very good boy! I hope your mom is as proud of you as I am of my son. Signed, Miriam."

"Miriam: You only call him once a week? Heck, my mom calls her therapist THREE times a week to tell him all about me. How about that?!?"

FORTY-ONE

Ana called in sick to work on her first day after the river trip. She wasn't physically sick . . . she was lovesick. To be in love with someone who didn't love you back was a horrible feeling. She stayed in bed all morning watching old Lifetime movies—which made it worse. Then she finally got up, drank some tea, and put on an old Linda Ronstadt record. She laid on the couch and listened to Linda sing exactly how she felt at the moment:

Well I spent my whole lifetime
In a world where the sunshine
Finds excuses for not hangin' 'round
I squandered emotions
On the slightest of notions
And the first easy loving I found
But soon all the good times
The gay times and play times
Like colors run together and fade
Oh Lord if you hear me
Touch me and hold me
And keep me from blowing away

There's times when I trembled
When my mind remembered
The days that just crumbled away
With nothing to show
But these lines that I know
Are beginning to show in my face

Oh Lord if you're listening
I know I'm no Christian
And I ain't got much coming to me

GARY HOPE

So send down some sunshine
Throw out your lifeline
And keep me from blowing away

FORTY-TWO

Dorothy went back to work a little depressed and a lot discouraged. Fortunately, there was plenty to do after being away for a week. One tourist received a snake bite last week and Dorothy had to fill out all the forms and medical releases. Another tourist had driven off road and gotten his Mustang stuck in a mud pit and threatened to sue the Park Service for damaging his car. However, the worst of all possible things happened last week as well . . . a tourist died.

A middle-aged, overweight man was by himself and drove to Grandview Point, where he got out of his car and got lost. Since he was alone no one really knew exactly what happened. They saw his car alone and locked in the parking area at Grandview Point, but he was nowhere to be seen. The following morning a search crew was called in and after about four hours they found his body deep in the canyon lying underneath a lone juniper tree. What was strange was that no predators had bothered the body. Not even the vultures had been around.

They traced his footprints around in circles, validating the fact that he was completely disoriented. He didn't have any water with him and was wearing loafers and dress pants. He apparently became confused and lost direction and wandered in circles all afternoon. It was unknown when he actually died, either that night or the next morning, but he chose a magnificent view as his final resting place. The juniper tree was the only tree on the plateau that looked out over a large canyon, with the river at the bottom. It was there he stopped, possibly to sit in the shade of the juniper, and gaze into the abyss for what would be his last memory.

The initial autopsy report stated heart failure, but who really knows. Dorothy read the report twice and nearly started crying. The man's nephew had come to identify the body and take his car.

The man was unmarried and had no children. The only thing that was known was that he chose an excellent place to sit down and breathe his last breath.

∽∽∽

When Dorothy came home that afternoon, she realized she really, really missed Noah. Maybe it was the after effects of the river trip, or the lyrics to the Linda Ronstadt song she couldn't stop singing, or maybe it was thinking about the dead man at Grandview Point . . . or all of them. Bottom line was that she had to write Noah again.

"My dearest Noah, I'm finally back home and have my computer problems solved. I hope you remember me after so long and will write me back. I've missed hearing from you. Please tell me what you've been doing while I was away. Always, your Ana."

When Noah saw and read that email, he could hardly sit still. In fact, he couldn't sit still. He finally got up and poured himself an Iron Maiden—he needed a stiff drink! He read the email fourteen times before he started typing the reply.

"Ana, my lovely, how do you think I could ever forget about you? All I do is think of you . . . what color your hair is, what color your eyes are, how tall you are, do you have freckles, how old you are, when you're coming to visit me? When ARE you coming to visit me? Or, don't you want to actually see me in person?"

Dorothy knew that Noah would eventually put her on the spot about them meeting in person. She wasn't sure how she would handle it. So, for now, she simply ignored that question and asked him, "You didn't tell me what you did all last week to amuse yourself while I was gone. Did you have any fun? Please tell me, I'm very interested."

"I'll tell you what I did, I MISSED YOU, ANA. That's what I did. But to fill in the hours while you were away, I went on a river trip down the Colorado."

"Oh, my, this wasn't the river trip you promised to take me on, was it? Remember, Noah, you promised to take me on a river trip in which we wouldn't need bathing suits and only one sleeping bag. Or have you forgotten that?"

"Oh, no, my dear. I would never forget that! This trip was with some friends here in Moab, and we all wore bathing suits all the time."

Dorothy knew that wasn't true; in fact, she was remembering when she saw him naked in the pool of water. Then she remembered when he saw her naked that last night in the river. The night he ignored her and started kissing Sandy . . . she wished she hadn't remembered that. It took her a few moments to get her bearings back, but then she wrote, "So it was just you and some of your buddies on this trip, huh?"

Noah didn't want to lie to Ana, but he didn't really want to tell the whole truth either, so he settled for, "Yeah, it was just some old friends from around town, a couple of the guys brought their girlfriends, but it was mostly just us guys."

"Did you bring a girlfriend, Noah?"

"Ana, my dear, you know that you're my girlfriend. I want to share a sleeping bag and swim without a bathing suit only with you . . . no one else."

"Noah, that is so sweet! Good to know that you did no nude bathing there without me and that you didn't see anyone nude either . . . right?"

Noah thought about his reply for a few moments, then wrote back, "No, of course not. The girls stayed with their boyfriends and the rest of us just fished some and messed around the fire at night. It was pretty boring really. I wish you had been there, Ana, there was no one else for me to really talk with."

Dorothy knew Noah was only trying to make her feel good, but still, it hurt her feelings a little for him to say he had no one to talk with. After all, she was there, she talked with him. She tried to sluff that off as she went into her kitchen to get a cup of hot tea. Before she came back to the computer, Noah had emailed again, "Ana, I'll make a deal with you. I'll send you a picture of me first so you can see what I look like. Then, you send me a picture of you. How about that? Please??"

Dorothy read that email and thought about her reply for so long that her tea was cold when she tried to drink it. She had to answer him . . . but how? She had to give him something, she couldn't keep putting him off every time he asked something of her. She finally typed back, "Okay, Noah, send me your picture first."

Noah looked all through his phone trying to find the most flattering picture of himself that was available. He finally settled on a picture of himself at a friend's wedding three years ago. He was wearing a suit and his hair was combed, but his smile was a little goofy. Oh, well, this one would do. He cropped it, enhanced it, and sent it to Ana. Now, all he could do was wait.

Dorothy looked at Noah's picture and wondered why he would send her a picture of himself with such a goofy-looking grin on his face. Maybe he thought he looked better in a suit than in shorts and tee shirt. She thought about sending him a phony picture of a pretty girl, but she knew she couldn't do that. Then she found a picture of herself from several years ago, standing on the beach, quite a distance away from her friend who took the picture. In fact, she was so far away, it was impossible to tell it was actually her in the picture. She started to send it—but no. She kept looking, then she found a picture of herself taken at a beauty salon last year. She had asked the beautician to take a picture of her from behind so she could see how her hair looked when she was standing up. Also, she had on her best tight-fitting blue jeans that really accentuated her behind, which was what she thought was her best feature.

She cropped the picture and lightened it a bit to highlight her legs, making sure her face could not be seen at all. When she was certain Noah would never be able to tell it was her, she sent it to him. Noah was so excited seeing an email with an attachment that he could barely click on the right spot to open it. When he finally opened it, he thought, "What the . . .!" Then he scanned down and saw those legs and her behind, and thought, "Oh, my, Ana . . . you've got a nice butt!" He enlarged it and rotated it but he still couldn't see her face. Dang!

He wrote her back confirming he received the picture and to inquire if she liked his picture, but he got no further reply from Ana. He printed the picture from his computer and enlarged it as much as he could. Then, later, he took it to bed with him and stared at it until he started getting drowsy. This was a major breakthrough! Tomorrow would bring more and better news . . . he was certain of it.

FORTY-THREE

It would prove to be a long workday for Noah. He kept checking his personal emails for a message from Ana, but nothing had arrived yet. Only work:

"Noah: My girlfriend is a little overweight, not much, but she has a little belly on her. She doesn't want to have sex with me because she said overweight girls tend to get pregnant easier. Is this true? Signed, Butch."

"Butch: I've consulted with all my doctor friends and they are of the consensus that the best things in life either make you fat, drunk or pregnant. So, yes, she might be right . . . or not."

"Noah: My grandpa had a heart attack about five years ago, but he's good now. The problem is that sometimes he takes these little nitroglycerin pills to help him. If he took one of these pills and tripped and fell down, would he blow himself up? Signed, Bart."

"Bart: He who knows nothing doubts nothing."

"Noah: If our bodies are 98.6 degrees temperature, then why do we feel so hot when it's only 90 degrees outside? Shouldn't we feel cooler? Signed, Cleve."

"Cleve: Watch out, you'll turn out ordinary if you're not careful."

"Noah: I have a personal question to ask. When I go for a doctor's visit, can he tell when I last had sex? Signed, no name."

"No name? I've been through the desert on a horse with no name . . . sorry, I got carried away for a moment. Umm, what was your question?"

"Noah: My wife's uncle drives me crazy. He argues with everybody all the time. Whenever we all get together, he makes it almost unbearable being around him. What can I do? Signed, Ryan."

"Ryan: My advice is to never argue with stupid people; they'll drag you down to their level and then beat you with experience."

"Noah: Once and for all--and quit beating around the bush--do you believe in evolution or that God created everything? Signed, Douglas."

"Douglas: The human body has 37,000,000,000,000 (that's 37 trillion) cells. Each cell is unique in its own way. Every human has different cells that make that particular human unique—we are all different. So, you're asking me if I think something like this evolved over time? Let me tell you a story, Douglas . . . early in the 1900s, an old farmer was driving his Model T down the road and it suddenly stopped on him. Broken down and he couldn't fix it or get it going again. After a few minutes a limousine came by and stopped. A thin, well-dressed man got out and asked him what was wrong. After talking to the farmer, the well-dressed man opened the hood, fiddled around a bit, then told the farmer to start the car. The farmer, only to be polite and having no confidence at all in this well-dressed man, did as he was asked. The car started up immediately. The farmer said, 'I never thought a man in a nice suit, with no grease on his hands, riding in a limousine would have the slightest clue of how to fix my car.' The well-dressed man replied, 'My name's Henry Ford. I created this car, I made all the parts, I know how it's supposed to work.'

And Douglas . . . that's my answer."

"Noah: I'm a single guy and I love to travel. The ocean, the mountains, the desert, I love them all. My dad is always getting on me about wasting my money just to escape my life—such as it is. Do you think he's right? Signed, Richard."

"Richard: The way I see things is that we travel not to escape life, but for life not to escape us."

"Noah: I graduated from nursing school and worked at a hospital for a while. Then I heard of a humanitarian group that travels to third world countries to give out free medical help. I joined this group. It drove my parents crazy that I would quit a great job with a great future to do this non-profit work. They think I'm lost and crazy and have no idea of what I'm getting myself into. But I feel drawn to this work and this organization. Do you think I'm crazy and lost, too? Signed, Kay."

"Kay: It feels good to be lost in the right direction, doesn't it?"

FORTY-FOUR

Dorothy stopped at her favorite coffee shop after work, the one where Noah didn't frequent, and she got a fresh cup of mocha latte as she thought about her dilemma. As she was sitting there, lost in thought, someone pulled out a chair next to her and sat down— Sandy, the river-rafting woman. Sandy said, "Mind a little company?"

Dorothy really didn't want any company, especially from Sandy . . . she still remembered Sandy kissing Noah the last night on the river. But, she replied, "No, hello, Sandy. How are you?"

Sandy answered, "Well, you know. So how did you like the river trip, girl?"

"It was great. Nice to get away for a few days. Thanks for getting me in the group."

"Let me ask you a question, Dorothy . . . how well do you know Noah? Remember him?"

"Yeah, he was on the river trip with us. I talked with him some in the raft, but other than that, I don't know him at all. Why?"

Sandy scrunched up her face a little, then said, "Well, that last night on the trip, we made out together for a while and I was wondering if he was seeing anybody right now."

This statement shocked Dorothy because she had always heard that Sandy was gay. She didn't know how she should answer this, so she lied, "I heard he was involved with a girl from out of town."

Sandy said, "You mean that girl he met online? Crap, that doesn't mean anything. Men are always trying to hook up with women online. Heck, I even do it some."

Dorothy wasn't sure if Sandy meant she tried to hook up with men or with women online. So, she tried to play it safe, "Other than that, I don't really know anything about him. Are you interested in him?"

Sandy smiled and replied, "I might be. He kisses really good and seems like a nice guy."

Dorothy had to nip this in the bud. She said, "Would you like me to ask around and see what I can find out?"

"Could you do that? Do you know people who would know?"

Dorothy nodded and said, "Yeah, I dated his best friend for a while." She guessed that one night she was with Duncan for forty-five minutes could count as a date. She continued, "I'll call him and he'll tell me everything he knows about Noah."

"Thanks, Dorothy. I'd just like to find out before I decide which way to go. Thanks for doing that."

Dorothy wasn't sure what Sandy meant by "which way to go," The more she thought about it, the more confused she became. Sandy thanked her again and gave Dorothy her email and phone number before leaving the coffee shop. Dorothy threw her mocha latte in the trash and got herself an expresso to sit and think about this. She didn't want to dig herself a hole so deep that she couldn't climb out.

When Dorothy got home, there was an email from Noah, "Ana, my dear, I love your picture. You're just as beautiful as I imagined—at least from the back. Would it be possible to see a picture of your face? I sent you my picture—did you like it?"

To buy herself some time, she found the picture of herself on the beach from about a hundred yards away and sent it to Noah. Then she turned the computer off and took a long, hot bubble bath.

Noah opened the picture Ana sent him, but, of course, he couldn't even tell if it was a man or a woman. He immediately wrote her back and waited for a reply. After three and a half hours of waiting, he decided to call it a night. He couldn't understand. Was Ana so ugly that she didn't want him to see her face? Maybe she was old. But she couldn't be too old, not judging from that picture of her butt. Or, maybe she only fourteen years old. He'd seen young girls who had mature bodies before—he felt a little creepy even thinking about this. Why would she intentionally keep hiding her face from him?

The next afternoon Dorothy emailed Sandy, "Sandy, I spoke with Noah's best friend, Duncan, and he said that Noah was indeed in an affair with this woman online and that they were meeting very soon. He said Noah was very taken with her and was hoping for great things. Sorry for the bad news. Hope to see you soon, Dorothy." Dorothy almost felt bad about lying to her friend . . . almost, but not quite.

Noah went to the Moab Brewery after work and immediately saw Duncan sitting by himself at the bar. He went over and sat next to him but Duncan never noticed him until Noah elbowed him. Duncan turned and looked at him but still didn't say anything. Noah asked, "What's wrong? Are you okay?"

"No, man, they're sending me back into the field next week. They promised I'd be around for a while, now they're sending me back to freaking Nevada."

"What's wrong with Nevada?"

"Have you ever been to Nevada?"

Noah thought about it and answered, "Yeah, I've been to Reno and Vegas."

"Well, they ain't sending me to Reno or Vegas. I'll be out in the middle of nowhere for at least three months while we do some drilling. It sucks!"

Noah asked, "Are you still seeing that young girl?"

"Nah, it didn't work out." Then Duncan looked at Noah and asked him, "Have you talked with that ranger, Dorothy, lately?"

Noah didn't want to tell Duncan about the river trip, so he lied to him, "No . . . I didn't really know her that well."

Just the opportunity Duncan was looking for to enhance his gigolo reputation, "Well let me tell you something about that girl, buddy . . . I tried to break it off with her but she wouldn't leave me alone. She kept calling me all last week, knocking on my door in the middle of the night, she's hard to satisfy."

Noah nodded and asked, "You're talking about the ranger, right? Dorothy?"

"Yeah, man, I told you she was a nymphomaniac. She's wearing me out!"

Noah continued to nod, knowing that he had caught Duncan in an out-and-out lie—Dorothy was on the river trip with him all last week. But he let his friend live in the moment and relish in his dreams. They shared a Black Raven Stout but after the story of Dorothy, Duncan slipped back into his depression—knowing he'd soon be leaving for desolate landscapes of Nevada.

ᎾᎾᎾ

Noah kept the two pictures of Ana on his nightstand. Each night, when he was in bed, he would hold the pictures and stare at them. The far-away picture did him no good at all. But there was something about the picture of Ana from behind. There was something that seemed almost familiar about it, he could nearly recognize something, but could never figure out exactly what that something was.

Dorothy didn't answer him the following day and he started to get a little worried, until the next morning when he had a message from her: "My dearest, Noah, I do love the picture you sent me. You are more handsome than I thought you would be. I bet all the girls in Moab are chasing you. That's why I hesitated to send you a picture of my face, Noah. I may not be as pretty as you would want in a new girlfriend. Your handsome face somewhat intimidated me. I would think someone like you would only be interested in beauty queens and fashion models. Am I right?"

"Ana, Ana, Ana . . . I thought you knew me better than that. It's YOU I'm interested in: your brains, your personality, your knowledge, your common sense, your humor, and, yes, your legs and behind are also a bonus. I think you probably underestimate yourself, Ana, I think you are a true beauty. Please send me something to look at. I promise, no picture will change our relationship or how I feel. You must believe me, Ana."

"Let me think about it, dear Noah. I must get to work now. I hope you have a great day out there in wild unknowns of Utah—be careful."

Noah also had to get busy, he was getting behind in his column. He needed to answer some questions from the good people of Salt Lake City, while he kept the image of Ana burned in his mind, as he tried to answer the question of what was gnawing at him about that picture.

FORTY-FIVE

"Noah: Why do they bury people six feet under? Why not eight feet, or ten, or four feet under . . . why six? Is there some significance to that? Signed, Pete."

"Pete: Several hundred years ago bodies were not buried in coffins, like today. They just put them in the ground, usually only eighteen inches deep, and covered them up. However, during the Black Plague, they were afraid the germs from the Plague might get to the surface, so they made the law to say six feet deep to keep any Black Plague germs from getting to the surface. And that's the truth, okay?"

"Noah: I was just wondering, how was the routine for milking cows discovered? Signed, Mac."

"Mac: By a very perverted farmer."

"Noah: I have a lot of plans when I graduate college. I keep telling my mom and dad all the things I want to do in the future, but I'm not sure they believe me or have confidence in me. I'll be the first one in our family to graduate from college, so that may be part of their problem. But I don't think it's wrong to shoot for the stars, do you? Signed, Riley."

"Riley: The greatest danger for most of us is not that our aim is too high and we miss it, but that it's too low and we reach it. Riley, keep going and don't stop till you're proud!"

"Noah: Is it our fault that the economy stinks? Are we to blame because the morals in this country suck? Are we, the ordinary citizens, the cause of all that's wrong in our country? Signed, Maurice."

"Maurice: No snowflake in an avalanche ever feels responsible."

"Noah: I'm having a sort of mid-life crisis. I'm thinking of quitting my job so I'll have time to find myself and be who I'm meant to be. I'm not married or have kids so my actions wouldn't harm anyone. But my friends think I'm crazy to even be considering this. What do you think? Signed, Grace."

"Grace: Life isn't about finding yourself. Life is about creating yourself."

"Noah: I think I just made a big mistake. My company offered me a promotion but I'd have to transfer to another state to take the new job. I like it here . . . I have friends and family and a comfortable life. But I'm having second thoughts now. I don't know if I'll ever get this opportunity again. Any thoughts? Signed, Jon."

"Jon: A ship is safe in the harbor, but that's not what ships are built for, is it?"

"Noah: My best friend, who shall remain nameless, really hurt me. I thought I could trust her with my secrets but I've found out she's telling everybody my private stuff. She has hurt me so badly I can never trust her again. How can I ever forgive her? Signed, Mary Jane."

"Mary Jane: I'm sorry to hear what your friend did to you. But my advice is to forgive her, not because she deserves forgiveness, but because you deserve peace."

"Noah: If you look at all the stars in the sky, it's almost impossible to believe we're the only life that exists in the entire universe, isn't it? What do you think? Is there life out there in the heavens? Signed, Carleton."

"Carleton: Sometimes I think we're all alone in the universe, and sometimes I think we're not. In either case, the idea is quite staggering . . . don't you think?"

"Noah: I wonder if you're as smart as you think you are. Are you? Signed, Mr. Average."

"Dear Mr. Average: I think I'm the wisest man alive, for I know one thing, and that is that I know nothing."

"Noah: I don't drink, not at all. But my friend Stanley does; he says it helps him remove stress. I don't believe this; I think he just says that so he can drink. What do you say? Does alcohol remove stress? Signed, Jordan."

"Jordan: I shouldn't tell you this because I don't know how old you are. But, it's true . . . alcohol does help remove stress . . . and bras . . . and panties."

FORTY-SIX

Noah and Ana emailed back and forth all week, Noah begging for a picture and Ana always putting him off. They discussed books, foreign cities, vacation spots, world affairs, religion, and everything else that interested them. Everything except when they would meet. Everything except where Ana lived and what Ana looked like . . . everything except the most important things Noah wanted to know.

He had planned a hike into the Double Arch Wilderness Region this weekend, but cloudy skies and the forecast of rain changed his mind. On Saturday morning, as the drizzle and rain began, he decided to go to Main Street and visit his favorite coffee shop and the Back of Beyond Bookstore to see if they had any new selections to choose from. His friend Duncan had gone off to the unknown, desolate wilds of central Nevada and Noah felt a little lonely. He was looking forward to sipping his coffee and watching the traffic go by the window on a leisurely Saturday morning.

His favorite table next to the window was open and he brought his blueberry muffin and coffee to sit and watch the rain. The wet weather would keep most of the tourists inside today or they would do their sightseeing from inside their cars. Noah had finished his muffin and was thinking about getting another one when he noticed Dorothy's vehicle come slowly down the street. He leaned over and watched as she parked down the next block, then he remembered that she liked the new coffee shop that just opened down there. He watched her get out and run into the coffee shop. He started thinking to himself. Sometimes, that's a dangerous thing for a lonely man to do when he sees a pretty girl by herself.

He abandoned his thoughts of a second muffin and threw his half-full cup of coffee into the garbage, then took off at a brisk walk towards the new coffee shop. It was now raining hard enough that Noah got pretty wet before he arrived. He went in and tried his best not to look around and see where Dorothy was. He was hoping she would see him and call out to him—she did see him, but didn't call out to him.

When he walked in, Dorothy almost got up and started for the restroom. Her hair was wet, and again, she had gone out without any makeup. She really didn't know what she should do. She wasn't actually "friends" with Noah. She had been on those hikes with him and on the river trip, and he had seen her naked, but . . .

While she was mulling over her options, Noah had gotten his coffee and turned to face her. He acted surprised to see her and raised his cup in an awkward form of hello. She waved him over to her table and smiled at him, trying to remember if she had brushed her teeth this morning. "Hey, Noah, pretty miserable day outside isn't it?"

"Yeah, I was going to hike the Double Arch Wilderness Area today until it started raining."

Dorothy tilted her head and replied, "Double Arch? I don't think I've ever been there. Is it nice?"

"I've only been there once and I didn't go far, it was late in the day, but from what I saw it was gorgeous."

Without even thinking, Dorothy said, "Let's go. You want to?"

Noah looked outside at the rain, which if anything was getting harder, then he remembered touching her leg that day, then he looked at her smiling at him and forgot everything else, before saying, "Yeah, let's go." He threw his fresh cup of coffee in the trash and said, "I'll go home and get my stuff. You can ride with me if you want to."

Dorothy was so excited she could hardly speak, but did say, "Okay, let me go home, change clothes, and I'll meet you back here in about thirty minutes."

Noah's mind was racing so fast he forgot to turn on his windshield wipers until he almost ran over a tourist from King of Prussia, Pennsylvania. Dorothy was being flooded with her own thoughts: Should I wear my short shorts in the rain? Should I put makeup on? Can anything be done with my hair in thirty minutes? They both ran in their respective houses, grabbed their hiking essentials and zoomed back to Main Street in less than twenty minutes. Neither of them gave a second thought to the rain, which was now pounding down on the little town of Moab, Utah.

Dorothy hopped in the front seat with Noah and he immediately took off before she could change her mind. It was about a thirty-minute drive out to the Double Arch Wilderness Area and both of them were quiet the entire drive. Noah was hoping she didn't change her mind because of the rain while remembering the vision of her walking out of the river nude that night. She was hoping the rain wouldn't change his mind, and she was also hoping that he remembered what she looked like as she walked naked out of the river that night.

They parked, they put on their raincoats and hats in the car, but neither of them mentioned the rain--it was a forbidden subject. Noah was in the lead since he had been on the trail before. It started off soggy, then went to muddy, then evolved into a small stream between the sandstone walls. Their feet disappeared into the watery trail with each step. But did either of them complain? Not on your life!

Soon, the trail started climbing, leaving the standing water behind. It was rising to about a thousand-foot elevation change from the parking lot. They were happy to start the climb, which would lead them to fantastic views of two large, hundred-foot, sandstone arches that were connected by a thick wall of rock. As they neared the summit of the climb, they both became thirsty; only then did it dawn on them that in their rush to get ready, they forgot to pack any water bottles.

Noah spotted a small overhang in the rock wall and quickly moved under the small, natural shelter. They both took their hats off and then looked at each other as Dorothy said, "Did you bring any water?"

Noah looked out at the pouring rain and answered, "Not a drop." They immediately started laughing at each other and the situation they were in. Off to the side of the overhang the water was dripping down in a steady stream. Dorothy cupped her hands to capture some of it, then slurped it up and nodded to Noah. He moved past her, lightly brushing against her front, and instead of cupping his hands to gather the water, he just tilted his head back under the stream and started drinking it straight off the rocks. Then Dorothy did the same thing, as they took turns gulping the streaming water and brushing against each other as they each took their turn. Water never tasted so good!

When they reached the trail's end, they were standing beneath the two massive sandstone arches. They could almost get completely out of the rain at one end of the largest arch. They stood there, staring out over miles and miles of uninhabited wilderness, each one not wanting to be anywhere else in the entire world at that moment. Almost instantly the rain stopped. Within a few minutes, the clouds dispersed and the sun broke through, instantly warming them. Noah thought how beautiful everything now looked. Dorothy thought, "Uh, oh . . . we don't have any water."

They found a nice boulder to sit on as they stared into a setting very people would ever see. Noah brought some almonds and peanut butter crackers out from his pack. Dorothy had a couple of granola bars and some pita bread—they both wished they had brought water. They talked about nothing and everything as they shared snacks. The memory of the nude river scene stayed firmly off-limits. Dorothy had on wilderness pants that unzipped just above the knee, turning them from full-length pants into shorts. Noah appreciated that gesture on her part. He remembered the day he accidentally touched her bare leg.

Now that the sun was out, Dorothy really wished she had put on some type of makeup—anything—but she hadn't. However, Noah thought she had put on makeup and wondered why the rain hadn't smeared it. As they started back down the trail, Noah immediately stopped and bent over to pick up something off to the side. He said, "Arrowhead," as he showed it to Dorothy.

She smiled and said, "Nice, you don't often see those out here."

Noah smiled and stuck the artifact in his pocket. Dorothy said, "You can't do that, Noah."

"Do what?"

"You can't keep that arrowhead. State law . . . you have to leave it where you found it."

Noah didn't make an attempt to get the arrowhead out of his pocket, and said, "Seriously?"

"Yes, seriously. It's against the law."

They both stared at each other momentarily, then Noah said, "You mean I have to put this back and let some tourist from Alamogordo find it and keep it?"

"It's against the law for him to keep it as well."

Noah said, "But nobody will know if HE keeps it."

Dorothy nodded and replied, "Maybe . . . but I'll know if YOU keep it."

Noah slowly put his hand in his pocket and brought out the arrowhead. He looked at it again and gently laid on the ground for a tourist from Alamogordo to find later. Dorothy said, "You're doing the right thing, Noah. Thank you."

They were both looking forward to the small overhang again so they could have some water, but when they arrived there, it was dry. That's the thing about the desert . . . it can pour down rain, then be dry as a bone thirty minutes later. By the time they reached the car, they were parched. If they'd had a siphon, they may have tried to drink some gasoline from the fuel tank. Dorothy said, "I think there's a gas station about halfway back to town."

Noah said, "I sure hope so. How in the world can two, fairly intelligent, college-educated, professional adults make such a stupid mistake?" They both laughed but they both knew why . . . they knew exactly why.

There was a gas station, just as Dorothy remembered. They bought large bottles of water and drank them in the shade of an old cottonwood tree. They sat side-by-side on a bench, not quite touching legs, but close . . . very close. When they made it back to town and Noah stopped to let Dorothy off at her car, she started to get out, then reached in her pocket and pulled out the arrowhead that Noah had found. She laid it on the dashboard in front of him and said, "If you ever tell anybody I did that, I'll kill you."

CCC

When Dorothy arrived back home, she threw her stuff in the washer and took a long shower. Then she poured herself a glass of wine and sat on the patio staring off into the distance. Her mind was racing all the way from the coffee shop this morning to when she laid the arrowhead on his dash this afternoon. As she poured a second glass of wine, she found herself, once again, questioning if she was pretty enough and good enough for someone like Noah.

Noah arrived at his home and threw his dirty clothes on the floor while he grabbed a beer from the refrigerator. He sat in front of the computer in his underwear and started to turn it on . . . but stopped. The thoughts in his mind were not of Ana and her emails. The thoughts he couldn't erase, and didn't want to forget, were of drinking rainwater off a rock, brushing against Dorothy, sitting under a cottonwood tree, almost, but not quite touching . . . he never wanted to forget that. So, he got up and put on some shorts and walked out to his patio to stare at the La Sal Mountains in the distance, while holding a beer in one hand and an arrowhead in the other.

FORTY-SEVEN

Noah wondered how he could concentrate on his work. Fortunately, he hadn't received any emails from Ana . . . fortunate because he didn't know how to answer them. He didn't know how to answer anything now, but he had to fulfill his obligations to the good people of SLC.

"Noah: I'm just starting my career after graduating from college. It's my first REAL job with a real company. I don't want to screw it up and I'm looking for some advice. I think if I start out great and don't make any mistakes, it'll make a great impression on them. Right? Signed, Keith."

"Keith: I understand your train of thought here. But let me give you a life example: The capital of Virginia is Norfolk, the capital of New York is Albany, the capital of California is Sacramento, the capital of Colorado is Denver, the capital of Kentucky is Frankfort, and the capital of Washington is Olympia. You're probably thinking, 'You made a mistake, Noah. The first one is wrong.' I made the first one wrong on purpose, Keith, because I wanted you to learn something important. This was for you to know how the world out there will treat you. All the rest of my answers are right, but you didn't congratulate me on those, did you? You only noticed the one I did wrong.

"That's the lesson, Keith. The world will never appreciate what you do right, it will only criticize you for what you do wrong. So, don't get discouraged! Always rise above the criticism. And always stay strong."

"Noah: What gets a smart guy like you excited? Signed, Lydia."

"Lydia: You're assuming a great deal there, but today I'm excited about everything. And as for being smart . . . I think the true sign of intelligence is not knowledge, but imagination. And, Lydia, right now my imagination is running wild."

"Noah: After you've lived your entire life and you know the end is near, how do you think you'll arrive at death's door? Will you be happy and satisfied with your life, or will you be sad by all you didn't accomplish? Signed, Juliette."

"Juliette: I love your name, it's graceful and beautiful. But to answer your intriguing question, I hope to arrive at death's door late, in love, and a little drunk."

"Noah: I have a serious question and I hope you'll give me a serious answer. We all have souls, though some may be better than others; however, do you think our souls influence what our bodies do? Or are our bodies completely independent from our souls? Signed, Jan."

"Jan: I'm going to answer your question with what I believe to be the truth. It's the only answer I can give you but I'm not sure it's the answer you're looking for. Jan, you don't HAVE a soul. You ARE a soul. You HAVE a body."

"Noah: My boyfriend and I recently broke up, then we became friends again—not dating, just friends. A lot of my girlfriends don't understand how I could be friends with him after the way he treated me, and they all hate him. I don't think that's right; he simply wanted to date someone else. I don't hate him for that. The opposite of love isn't hate, is it, Noah? Signed, Christine."

"Christine: I'd love to meet you someday. I agree with you, the opposite of love isn't hate. It's selfishness."

"Noah: My brother-in-law is a nice guy. That's the problem—he's too nice! He doesn't dislike anything; nothing seems to get him riled up. I have no idea what he stands for because he never says what's on his mind. I'm sure he's never made an enemy in his entire life. I'm not complaining about him; I just think it's weird. Do you? Signed, Ernest."

"Ernest: Show me a man with no enemies and I'll show you a man who's never stood for crap!"

"Noah: I've found that it's no use arguing with my wife about anything. I'll never win. When I was younger, we'd have some arguments that were real doozies. But you know what? It wasn't worth it. Even if I won, it wasn't worth it. I'd like to tell all the married people out there what I learned—it's not worth arguing about. Signed, Hillis."

"Hillis: You are a wise man. My uncle always told me, 'Noah, if you're wrong and you shut up, you're wise. But if you're right and you shut up, you're married.'"

"Noah: I'm in a deep funk and need some positive remarks. I just lost my scholarship at college (long story) and my part-time job, which was with the school. I had to give my mom the money I had saved to help her with some medical bills and now I have nothing. No education, no job, and no money. Pretty sad, isn't it? Signed, Mack."

"Mack: I'm sorry. Sometimes God will put a Goliath in your life for you to find the David within you . . . and you can."

FORTY-EIGHT

Dorothy was back at work at Canyonlands National Park, answering all the same questions that the tourists ask a hundred times a day while trying to keep a smile on her face: Where is the nearest Coke machine? Where is the bathroom? Are there any rattlesnakes out here? How long does it take to see everything? She was used to it, but sometimes . . .

She decided that when she got home later that afternoon she would email Noah, as Ana. She couldn't keep living like this; she needed some sort of resolution. When she got home, she didn't even take off her ranger uniform, she went straight to the computer. She knew exactly what she wanted to say in her email: "Dearest, Noah, I'm sorry for not writing sooner. I had a lot on my mind and I needed to think of how to ask you what I want to ask you. Noah, I want you to be perfectly honest with me when you answer these questions. Sometimes we joke with each other and are playful but I need to know exactly, truthfully how you feel. I want you to be honest and answer this: In the town where you live, is there not a single woman there who you are attracted to? Isn't there anyone who interests you—at least physically? There must be someone who you find attractive and interesting. I need to know your honest feelings, Noah. I truly want to know what you find attractive in a woman. If there is a woman there who interests you, please let me know. That's all I'm asking. Don't I deserve an honest answer? Please?

Ana"

Dorothy had no idea how Noah would answer her questions. She truly did not know if he was attracted to her or to the illusion of his imaginary friend, Ana. After she sent the email, she tried doing some housework, while keeping the computer on to see if Noah wrote back. She finally gave up on the housework and just got a glass of wine and sat in front of the computer waiting. It would be quite a wait because Noah was out helping a friend with his mountain biking company. His friend had a dozen people out riding the famous Slickrock Bike Trail and his van that hauled all the bikes out to the trail had broken down. He asked Noah to go by his office and pick up the spare van and drive it out to him. He knew Noah would help him, and Noah did.

After all the tourists had been rescued, and the bikes had been stored away, Noah and his friend dropped by the Moab Brewery so his friend could buy him dinner for helping him out. Of course, as with all single men, the conversation quickly resorted to the question of women. Noah's friend, Chip, filled Noah in on his latest escapades with women and of all the pretty tourists he'd had over the last few months. Noah never knew whether to believe Chip or not. Tourists were known to do some crazy things, but Chip also had the reputation as a good storyteller. And, of course, all men were known to brag, especially where women were involved.

After Chip ran out of stories, he asked Noah what was new with him. Who was he seeing? Who did he want to hook up with? Since Chip was a friend, but not a close friend, Noah thought he might be a good person to really explain his situation to—if that was possible. So, he began: "Chip, something really weird has happened to me. I met this woman online and have fallen for her. The problem is that I've never met her, don't know where she lives, and honestly, I don't really know her name. She goes by Ana and we've really connected with each other. Even though I've never met her, I feel like I want to marry her! Sounds crazy doesn't it?"

Chip set his beer down, picked up a potato chip, and said, "You're kidding, right?"

"No, I'm not. We email all the time and we both love the same things, and sometimes she gets me so excited I don't know what I'm doing. She's really special."

Chip ate the potato chip and replied, "But you've never seen her?"

"Nope."

"Aren't you afraid she might be ugly? Or old? Or . . . ugly?"

Noah nodded and took a moment to answer, then said, "I don't think she is. I don't know why I think that, I just don't. She sent me a picture of her back—not her face—so I know she's not fat, but that's all I know."

"Well, Noah, if a girl doesn't send you a picture of her face, that means something . . . she's UGLY!"

"Most times I would agree with you, but not this time. I don't know why she won't send me her picture, but I'm positive, I'm really certain, that she's pretty. I just know it, Chip."

Chip took a long drink from his mug, then said, "Well, find her and go see her, then you'll know if she's what you want."

"That's the problem, Chip. I'm not really sure if she IS what I want."

"I thought you said you might be in love with her."

"Yeah, I did say that."

"But . . . "

Noah had to gather his thoughts before he responded to that "But." He finally said, "But, I may have met someone else. Someone I can't quit thinking about. Someone I think I'd really like to spend time with. Someone who lives here in Moab."

This really got Chip's attention. "Who? Anybody I know?"

"She works out at Canyonlands and her name is Dorothy. She lives over near the river."

Chip looked up toward the ceiling for a moment, then said, "Is she the ranger with the nice legs and cute butt? Sorry, I didn't mean it like that, Noah."

Noah smiled and answered, "Yeah, no problem, that's the way I describe her, too. I've seen her a few times on hikes and we were on a river trip together. She just gets to me . . . you know what I mean?"

Chip said, "Was that the river trip a couple of weeks ago where I heard that old Sandy got drunk and passed out?"

"Yeah, that's the one. She got naked too—course we all did."

Chip's mouth dropped open, and he said, "Y'all got naked? Really?"

Noah smiled and answered, "Yep, we all jumped in the river that last night and things got crazy." He started to tell Chip that Sandy started kissing him, but quickly decided to omit that small fact.

"Well, if the ranger was there, did she get naked too?" When Chip asked this, he leaned forward so he wouldn't miss Noah's answer.

"Oh, yeah. She got naked just like everybody else. And let me tell you something, Chip, even in the dark and under the water, she still looked incredible."

All Chip could say was, "Dang!"

They both stared at their empty beer mugs for a moment thinking about the vision of Dorothy naked in the river. Then Chip asked, "Whatcha gonna do?"

"I was hoping you could help me decide."

Chip sighed and said, "I can't even handle one girl, dude. I have no idea how to deal with two of 'em."

ᘓᘓᘓ

Noah made it home and was totally surprised to find an email from Ana waiting on him. On one hand, he was very excited to see what the email said, but on the other hand, he was filled with trepidation over what the email might say. When he finally read the message, he sat back and thought to himself, "I have no idea how to answer those questions." He didn't want to lose his relationship with Ana, but how could he reign in the emotions he was feeling for Dorothy. At least with Ana, he knew she liked him back—a lot. With Dorothy, he wasn't entirely sure. Yes, they had a good time; yes, she seemed to enjoy his company . . . but was she just being polite? He truly didn't know. There was no way he could jeopardize his relationship with Ana just because he was giddy with Dorothy. But he also didn't want to lie to Ana and tell her that NO ONE in the entire town of Moab interested him. That would almost be impossible if not downright unmanly.

He wrote one email, then deleted it. Soon, he wrote another one and deleted it. Then the third email was deleted as well. He finally closed the computer and thought he'd better sleep on this. Hopefully, in the morning he would have some clearer understanding of what he should say. He certainly hoped so.

FORTY-NINE

Answering some work emails in the morning helped Noah clear his mind temporarily:

"Noah: Several people have asked you this over the years and yet you never answer them. We want to know! Can you please give us a clue? How old are you, Noah? Signed, Judy."

"Judy: Okay, here's your clue: When I was a boy the Dead Sea was only sick."

"Noah: I work as a secretary in a big firm. I know it's a nowhere job. I went to night school to get an associate degree but it never helped me get a better job. Now I'm thinking of maybe getting a four-year degree at night to see if that will help me advance. I just don't know. It would take so long to finish everything, I'm not sure it's worth the effort. I need some encouragement, Noah . . . if there is any. Signed, Brooke."

"Brooke: Nice to hear from you. Don't get discouraged. Coca Cola only sold twenty-five bottles its first year. Never give up! You'll be glad someday that you didn't."

"Noah: Do you watch the evening news? If you do, please tell me which show I can watch that doesn't have any crybabies, winey adults, or holier-than-thou, pseudo-intellectuals spouting off their version of the so-called news. It's sickening what they're doing. Signed, Eddie."

"Eddie: I wish I could. Most younger people will have trouble believing this, but there was once a guy named Walter Cronkite who would read the news on television every night. He didn't seem to have an agenda or try to make anybody look bad or good. He would just read the news and then, get this . . . we would all just make up our own minds about what we thought. He didn't interview smarmy, opinionated, talking heads; he just read the news, matter-of-factly, and then he would just sign off and shut up. I'm not making this up, Eddie."

"Noah: I think I'm a smart guy. I should be graduating from college soon and I think I can make a difference in the world—I really do! In your opinion, where should I concentrate my efforts to have the best effect? What area of the world needs the most help? That's where I want to concentrate my efforts. Thanks, Ivan."

"Ivan: Don't ask what the world needs. Ask what makes you come alive, and go do it! Because what the world needs is people who have come alive."

"Noah: I've had two failed marriages and a few broken relationships. I'm not sure this 'love' thing is for me. I'm just not good at it. I know how you feel about love—I've been reading your columns—but, certainly, you don't think love is the answer for everybody do you? Some people are just different and need different things from life. I know you won't agree with this, but it is possible, Noah. Signed, Jill."

"Jill: I don't agree. As far as I'm concerned, love is the bridge between you and everything."

"Noah: I need some help. The state has cut off my Food Stamps allotment. My unemployment checks have run out and my free medical services have been restricted. Do you know of any other state or national social programs I can apply for? I like it here; there's lots to do and I don't want to move away, but I need some help. Thanks, signed, Tim."

"Tim: Unless you're disabled, or old, or totally unable to work, I've found that the best social program is a job."

"Noah: I'm exhausted by how stupid everyone is getting. I read your column every day and I can't believe some of the questions people ask you. Is common sense a thing of the past? Are people so dumbed down now that they can't think for themselves? What is going on with our country, Noah? How do you put up with all of it? Signed, Michelle."

"Michelle: You never know when one kind act or one word of encouragement will change a life forever."

"Noah: Do you believe what the Bible says, that money is the root of all evil? Signed, Sandra."

"Sandra: The Bible doesn't actually say that. The Bible says the LOVE of money is the root of all evil. However, sometimes I feel that the lack of money may be the root of all evil."

"Noah: I can't dance at all. Do you know of a good dance school where I can learn? It would make my girlfriend very happy. Thanks, Roberto."

"Roberto: You don't need a dance school . . . just listen to 'Mustang Sally' by Wilson Pickett. Trust me, you'll start dancing."

FIFTY

Noah finally decided he could not tell Ana the whole truth concerning the question of whether there was anyone that he found attractive. He definitely didn't want to hurt her feelings and he wanted her to know how special she was to him. So, he wrote, "Dearest Ana, you know how I've always felt about you. Certainly, there are some attractive women here in Moab. I'm not going to act crazy and say that I've never noticed any—that would be insane. However, there are no other women that I would rather talk to, and be with, and communicate with, than you. We have something that can't accurately be described . . . heck, I can't even describe it to my friends. But to answer your question, no, there is no one here that interests me nearly as much as you do. The question now is: What do we do about that?

Please let me know,

Noah"

Dorothy read the email several times just to make sure she didn't interpret anything the wrong way. It seemed to her that Noah was saying there was no one in Moab that interested him as much as Ana. That's what she was afraid of. The times Noah spent with her on the hikes, the river trip, and in the rain were just his way of passing time until he could meet his dream girl—Ana. In her mind, she was not Noah's dream girl . . . she was only there occupying his time. He truly wasn't interested in her. Now, her question was: What do I do now?

Dorothy thought now might be the right time to transfer to another national park. After all, that was her plan from the beginning—to see and experience the United States by working in various parks across the country. She'd never been to California, and they had several parks there that were all gorgeous with good reputations. Maybe Montana or Washington . . . there were several parks that started her mind wandering. The only thing she was certain of was that she couldn't stay here and risk running into Noah. Moab was such a small little town that she could never completely avoid seeing him. She decided to start filling out transfer forms in the morning. She could fill out several of them and see which ones had openings available. Usually, they all did.

Once again, she decided to cease her email communications with Noah, now that she was 100% certain that she was not the girl Noah wanted. She didn't want to stop, but why keep torturing herself? Why keep him in the dark? Let him move on and finally find someone he'd be happy with. Then she went to her bed and cried.

Noah kept a vigil with his computer, but no answers came from Ana. He wrote another email which also went unanswered. He didn't have a good feeling about things. Eventually, he too went to his bed and held the arrowhead in one hand and the picture of Ana in the other. He stared at the picture trying to understand what it was that couldn't quite click in his mind. It was as if the picture was trying to tell him something and he couldn't understand what it was saying.

It was a long, depressing work week for Noah. The rain had persisted, making each day drizzly and uncomfortable. Add that to the fact that he had no emails from Ana to look forward to and his life was now bordering on drudgery. On Saturday morning he decided to go back to Main Street and sit in his favorite coffee shop and watch for Dorothy. He sat there from 8:30 until noon Saturday and became thoroughly saturated with coffee. He never saw Dorothy or her vehicle.

Dorothy moped around her house Saturday morning. She didn't even take her pajamas off until after 12:00 when her phone rang. It was her friend Sandy asking if she wanted to go to the Brewery with her that night. Dorothy didn't really want to, but Sandy was persistent and eventually they agreed to meet there about seven that evening. Since tourist season was winding down a little, the crowds there wouldn't be too bad anymore. Her only concern was that she knew Noah liked going there as well, but since she'd be with Sandy, she'd be okay.

After the coffee shop, Noah went home and took a nap, which was pretty amazing with all the caffeine he'd consumed. He called his friend Chip later but got no answer. He didn't want to cook, he didn't want to watch television, he didn't want to do anything—except drink—not coffee. So he got dressed and started for the Brewery. He found a seat at the far end of the bar where he would not be disturbed by the comings and goings of any locals or tourists. He ordered a Black Raven Stout and took his first sip from the frothy foam when he saw Sandy and Dorothy walk in the front door. His first thought was, "Oh, no, I hope Sandy doesn't see me." Almost immediately, Sandy waved to him.

She said to Dorothy, "There's Noah over there; let's go say hello to him. You heard he tried to screw me on the river trip, didn't you?"

Dorothy pulled her arm as she started to walk away and said, "What? He tried to screw you? Really?"

Sandy smiled and said, "Yeah, he was all over me, but to be honest, I'd just broken up with my girlfriend and I just wasn't into men right then. But if he's interested tonight, I might just leave you here by yourself—if you catch my drift." Then she started over to Noah, leaving Dorothy standing there in a daze.

By the time Dorothy made it over to them, Sandy and Noah were laughing at something. Sandy ordered a beer and said, "I got to go pee. I'll be right back."

Noah and Dorothy stared at each other. Then Dorothy couldn't help herself, she asked, "You tried to screw Sandy?"

Noah almost choked on his beer before answering. "What? What are you talking about?"

"Sandy said you tried to screw her on the river trip."

Noah shook his head in wonder and said, "That girl is crazy! She swam up behind me in the river that night and then started kissing me before I even knew who it was. When I saw it was her, she pulled away and puked in the river, then passed out. It was all we could do to get her to shore and put her in her tent."

Dorothy smiled and said, "I should've known better . . . I know how she is. Sorry I asked that."

Noah smiled back and almost made Dorothy faint. She played with the top button of her blouse and almost made Noah faint. Before either of them actually passed out, Sandy came back and said, "Where's my beer?"

The bartender brought her beer over and Sandy said, "We're getting a table over there Noah. Come join us if you want to."

Noah wanted to sit with Dorothy, but definitely not with Sandy, so he said, "I might catch you later. You girls have fun."

Sandy slapped him on the back and started to kiss him full on the lips, but Noah turned away to absorb the kiss on his cheek near his ear. Dorothy smiled and arched her eyebrows as Sandy said, "Let's go girl and leave this hunk for another time." They turned to walk over to an empty table near the window and Noah watched Dorothy walk away. As he watched her walk, his mind went blank—in a good way.

He thought, "From behind, she almost looks like the picture I have of Ana." Before he could process that thought any longer, the girls sat down. Dorothy made a point of facing out the window so she wouldn't be distracted by Noah sitting at the bar. When she sat down, Noah thought, "Her hair looks a lot like Ana's hair from behind." His mind went blank again as his senses were trying to comprehend all they had experienced.

He decided to go to the bathroom and then slip out the exit door without Sandy seeing him. All the way home his mind was whirling over what he'd seen. He couldn't concentrate on television so he played a few old records he had—music could always make him forget everything, or even worse, make him remember everything. He consciously tried to think back to his Salt Lake City days, to remember the girls he dated there. Then he tried to go back even further to his college days and relive some of those escapades . . . however, his mind kept returning to his conversations with Dorothy on the river trip. Inadvertently touching her thigh on the hiking trip. Having coffee with her and watching her smile. The hiking trip in the rain, brushing up against her, sitting side-by-side on the picnic table, not quite touching each other, but close enough to feel the electricity. Maybe listening to John Lennon sing "Girl" was not such a good idea after all.

He tried to read the latest CJ Box novel in bed but couldn't concentrate. He put the book down and picked up the arrowhead and the picture of Ana from behind. Dorothy in one hand, Ana in the other. Each holding a special place in his heart. Each one separate, each one unique, each one apparently unobtainable. Before turning the light off, he held up the picture of Ana again, comparing it to his memory of Dorothy earlier tonight. Same shapes from behind. Same color hair, similar cuts. Back and shoulder shapes very close. Legs seem to be the same length, butt seems to be shaped the same—or is he imagining this because he wants Ana to look like Dorothy. Now he's really confusing himself. Best to set the arrowhead down, put the picture back in the nightstand drawer, and turn off the light before his brain implodes.

Dorothy didn't notice Noah had left the Brewery until she visited the restroom. She looked all around without being too obvious about it. Just another case in point to prove that Noah was not interested in her at all. He had every opportunity to come and sit with them for dinner, yet he chose not to. Now she had to endure the rest of the evening watching Sandy flirt with every single man and woman who came in the bar. When the night was finally over, she went home to her computer, not to write a message to Noah as she had been doing for the last several months, but to review her applications for transfer to another national park. She had narrowed her choices down to Rocky Mountain National Park, Sequoia National Park, or Death Valley National Park. Death Valley seemed the most appropriate at this time in her life. She emailed her application to each of them and would now wait to see if there were any available openings.

She went to bed and turned the light off but couldn't sleep. She kept remembering all the emails of the past when she and Noah would flirt with each other. She remembered the electricity of his hand absently touching her thigh on that one hiking trip. She relived every conversation they had on the rafting trip. And, what hurt the most, was she could not forget how she felt on the last hiking trip in the rain—how special that was. How she wanted to feel like that forever. Then she started crying because she would never feel that way again.

FIFTY-ONE

Noah tried to do some work but his heart wasn't in it. His first email from work was,

"Noah: Our street doesn't have but one streetlight on the entire block. This is a major safety hazard and allows the criminal element to lurk around freely. Can't something be done about this? Signed, Duncan."

"Duncan: Do you think I care about your streetlight?"

He deleted this before sending it to the paper. He tried a few others but deleted them all. He'd have to do double duty tomorrow—or else get sued by all the Duncan's of the world.

The weather had cleared up enough for him to dry off his chair and sit outside and stare out into the desert. No matter which direction he looked, all he saw was Dorothy's face to the left and Ana's picture to the right. He went inside and brought the picture of Ana and the arrowhead outside with him. He stared at the picture and said, "Ana, what happened to us? What went wrong? Do I just let you go without a fight? What do I do? Help me, please!"

Then he picked up the arrowhead and spoke to it: "Dorothy, if things were different I'd chase you to the moon and back. You remind me so much of my Ana. You both have the same hair, the same legs, the same body . . . everything. Why does life have to be so hard?" He alternated his attention from the arrowhead to the picture. Each time he gazed at the picture his mind began questioning itself—almost as if it were in a different universe. His mind asked the question, "What if Ana and Dorothy were the same? They look alike, they act alike—why couldn't they merge into one being? Or, maybe the love gods HAVE combined them both . . . it's possible."

Noah wanted it to be possible, he really did. It was a nice dream. He kept staring at the picture, then he would close his eyes and draw up the vision and memory of Dorothy. Why did he keep coming back to this same issue? Why? Because they were so similar, that's why. Then he started questioning himself and all his emails to Ana.

Why wouldn't she tell him where she actually lived?

Why wouldn't she send him a picture of her face?

Why was she so secretive about her life?

Then, the $64,000 question . . . could Ana and Dorothy actually be the same person? Could that be possible? It's not impossible! The more he ran this through his mind, the more probable it became. By noon, he had almost convinced himself that it had to be true. But how would he know for sure?

∽∽∽

Dorothy received an immediate response from Death Valley National Park. Yes, they were very interested in her resume and application. They invited her to come out there and meet everyone to see if that's truly what she wanted? After all, Death Valley was not the most sought-after park job in the country. It was hot, hotter, and hottest of any national park in America. Usually, only the rangers who had gotten into trouble and were on probation got stationed there. They seldom had anyone volunteer for the job. "Yes," she emailed back and told them she could make the drive over on the next weekend. At least it would get her out of town so she wouldn't bump into Noah or Sandy for a while.

Noah had a plan. He didn't want to wait until the next weekend to try and catch Dorothy somewhere in town. He drove out to Canyonlands where she worked and parked in the small lot at the offices. There were a few other tourist cars there as well, which would help with his plan. He saw Dorothy's vehicle parked in the back, so he knew she was there. He stood at the door and looked in the window but didn't see her up front; she must be back in her office. That was even better!

He went in and mingled with the other tourists among the pamphlets and books and souvenirs. He wore an old floppy hat pulled down low over his face in order to disguise himself, and he stayed away from the door to the offices. He hoped he wouldn't have to wait too long for Dorothy to come out. After twenty minutes, she did come out holding some papers in one hand. Noah walked to the other end of the book rack and waited to see what she would do.

Dorothy placed her papers in a folder and turned to walk back to her office when Noah said in a loud voice, Ana." Dorothy didn't stop or flinch, so he called out again, "Ana!!" She never reacted. Four more steps and she was back in her office. Noah knew—HE KNEW—this would work. He knew if he called out Ana, that she would stop and turn around. But, she didn't. Dorothy wasn't his Ana. His dream ended so suddenly that he didn't realize he was blocking an old woman from Kansas City from the book rack. She tapped him on the shoulder, startling him. He apologized and slowly shuffled out the door.

Dorothy went back in her office and took out her earbuds so she could make a phone call. She loved listening to old Linda Ronstadt songs on her headphones. This particular song, "I'm So Lonesome I Could Cry," was a little too close to home for her. She always wore her earbuds in the office so she didn't hear the clutter and noise all the tourists made outside her door. She dialed the number and absently looked out her window to see a vehicle that looked exactly like Noah's leaving the parking lot. That was strange.

Noah made the hour-long drive back to Moab in a fog. He had been completely convinced Ana and Dorothy were one in the same. He was brokenhearted, crestfallen, and miserable on the drive back.

಄಄಄

He went back to work answering the questions from the good people of Salt Lake City. For a few days, his answers were so depressing and morose that his editor called to ask if he was okay. He was not okay. He finally got up enough strength to visit the Brewery the next Friday night, only to find Sandy at the bar with an older lady Noah had never seen before. After hellos were made, Sandy said, "I guess you heard Dorothy's gone."

This news stunned Noah. He didn't answer, he could only stare at Sandy, hoping she was playing with him. She continued, "She's starting a new job somewhere in California. I guess we weren't hip enough for her out here in the middle of nowhere." Before Sandy could continue, Noah turned around and walked back out the door.

He didn't know what to do or think. In fact, he couldn't think. Ana and Dorothy were now both gone from his life. He had nothing left. He wanted and needed a magical solution to his problem, yet he refused to believe in magic.

The smartest man in the world (except for Conrad, Dickie, Jerry, Mark, Jon, and Allen) edited this book for me. I'm assuming he did an admirable job but since I have no idea where or how commas or semi-colons should be applied, I'm only guessing. However, I appreciate all his hard work and the hours he put in to make the text presentable and readable.

Thanks, Larry.

Ana is the eighth novel from Gary Hope. Two previous books have won national awards from the Online Book Club of America. Gary finds inspiration for his books from his many travels, as is the case with *Ana*. His travel experiences in Moab, Killarney, Galway, Dubrovnik, Seattle, Venice, Iceland, St. Petersburg, Malta, London, Nassau, Red Springs, and Hawaii have given him a perspective on life and love that helps create lifelike characters that readers can identify with.

www.ingramcontent.com/pod-product-compliance
Lightning Source LLC
Chambersburg PA
CBHW070819180626
46818CB00001B/323